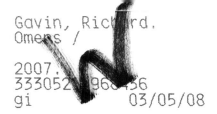

RICHARD GAVIN

MYTHOS BOOKS LLC

POPLAR BLUFF

MISSOURI

2007

Mythos Books LLC
351 Lake Ridge Road,
Poplar Bluff,
MO 63901
United States of America

www.mythosbooks.com

Published by Mythos Books LLC 2007

FIRST EDITION

Cover art and copyright © 2007 by Harry O. Morris.

All stories and foreword copyright © 2007 by Richard Gavin.

The author asserts the moral right to
be identified as the author of this work.

ISBN-13: 978-0-9789911-2-8
ISBN 10: 0-9789911-2-5

Set in *Tibetan Beef Garden* & *Adobe Garamond Pro.*

Tibetan Beef Garden by Astigmatic One Eye Typographic Institute.
www.astigmatic.com

Adobe Garamond Pro by Adobe Systems Incorporated.
www.adobe.com

Typesetting, layout and design by PAW.

ACKNOWLEDGEMENTS

—In the Shadow of the Nodding God—
Originally appeared in *Shadow Writers.*

—The Pale Lover—
Originally appeared in *Poe's Progeny.*
Gray Friar Press. Gary Fry, ed.

—Strange Advances—
Originally appeared in *Darkness Rising.*
Prime Books. Maynard & Sims, ed.

—What Blooms in Shadow Withers in Light—
Originally appeared in *Halloween 3.0*
Cyber-Pulp. Bob Gunner, ed.

—A Form of Hospice—
Originally appeared in *Horrors Beyond.*
Elder Signs Press. William Jones, ed.

] [

] ALL OTHER MATERIAL IS ORIGINAL TO THIS COLLECTION [

] [

This book is for J. P. Drapeau
and for Errol Undercliffe

CONTENTS

Darkness can be a source of elation.

A peculiar bliss seems to bloom within the cellar of the psyche; that abyss of submerged consciousness. All of us have experienced these joys at one time or another, perhaps through the delirium of a fever dream, or via artistic horrors. Such excursions into our inner darkness disrupt the tedium of life by administering to us a dose of *otherness*—a force that, according to our present understanding of the human condition, simply should not be.

On the printed page or the silver screen this *otherness* might take the form of a walking cadaver eager to gorge on the blood of the living. In our dreams it may guise itself as a cyclopean temple or an abandoned house hidden in some primeval wood. But no matter what shape this *otherness* assumes, our encounters with it are significant and therefore should be cherished. The shadows of the mind hold profound truths. They afford us insight into the mysteries that dwell both within and beyond the flesh. Such insights disturb rather than comfort us. For instead of reinforcing our preconceived reality construct, *otherness* shatters our cozy little psychic womb, leaving us defenceless and utterly exposed to primordial chaos. (I am reminded of Nietzsche's eloquent observation from *Beyond Good and Evil*: "All great things must first wear terrifying and monstrous masks in order to inscribe themselves on the hearts of humanity.")

So despite the fact that the majority of our species chooses to avoid any encounters with the strange and the macabre, the universe *demands* that each one of us, willingly or not, enters that labyrinth of the subconscious.

The most common conduit for this process, one that crosses all boundaries of culture and age, is the nightmare.

Nightmares are a universal component of the human condition. And I for one am a firm believer that the nightmare is a fleeting glimpse into a rich and vital dimension of consciousness.

Of course if one takes into account the sundry anxieties of modern life, one would of course be foolish to assume that *all* nightmares are the by-products of the universe trying to pass on some form of teaching. In fact, many of the dreams that cause us to jolt awake or leave us breathless and disoriented in the dead of night are little more than psychological flotsam; a kind of psychic residue left over from the frenzy of workaday existence. Indeed a large percentage of our nightmares can be attributed to an unpaid credit card bill or a misplaced set of keys than to any sort of transcendentalism. Nevertheless, there is a small and very precious class of nightmare, one whose overwhelming *otherness* propels it beyond the scope of the mundane mental baggage we lug into our dreams.

I refer to these profound dream terrors as Gnostic Nightmares.

An example of the Gnostic Nightmare might be: *"In the dream I was wandering through my grandmother's house, except that I knew it wasn't my grandmother's house. It looked just like it, but something told me that this wasn't her house at all. It was as if I had somehow stumbled into a forbidden chamber... "*

Of course the 'grandmother's house' imagery is simply a reflection from one's pool of personal memories, a handle that one can cling to until they get their bearings within the dreamscape. But that *tangible current* that informs the dreamer that this is most assuredly *not* their grandmother's house is the very essence of the Gnostic Nightmare. This feeling—a blend of awe and dread—occurs when one realizes that they are not in control of their mental surroundings. In such moments we suddenly wonder if it is we who are dreaming, or if we are *being dreamed*. This is a sensation that utterly fascinates me.

Disorientation is a common symptom of the nightmare. Perhaps this is because in such dreams we are only ever able to comprehend the elements that appear in our immediate dream vicinity. Everything outside the boundaries of our vision remains concealed by darkness, unknowable, untrustworthy. And while we can hardly consider ourselves to be omniscient in everyday life, even the meagre gauges we use to make our lives seem somewhat cohesive; i.e. logic, the laws of cause and effect, the certainty of our own identities, are useless in the nightmare. Like babes in the woods, we are forced to wander without the benefit of our usual armour.

The Gnostic Nightmare plays like an extended instance of déjà vu; tilting all our perceptions until the whole of our being is unstable and askew. Though we may become lucid in our nightmares, and hence recognize that what we are experiencing is a harmless vision, we are still awed by the knowledge that the world we are traipsing through is much larger and more perilous than we are able to perceive at any given moment. The knowledge that we are in a *"house that looks just like Grandmother's house"* turns dreadful the minute we know that there is *"something"* about the house that can only be hinted at. Its true and complete face remains hidden.

This veiled glimpsing of vast truths connects the nightmare with the horror story.

One of the great trade secrets of macabre literature is that in any effective tale, the supernatural element (or elements) must always be larger than their appearance within the tale itself. An author may introduce vast supernatural forces into a plotline, but the author may never (and, in all likelihood, *can* never) fully explain these forces. For example, a writer can craft a thoroughly chilling and convincing haunted house story without having to resort to an in-depth analysis of how hauntings occur. The reader can relish the *effects* of a haunting even when the author decides to forego a pseudoscientific explanation at the tale's conclusion.

In Shirley Jackson's *The Haunting of Hill House* we come to know a little bit about Hugh Crain (the deranged creator of the titular mansion), and the insidious impact the house has on its visitors, but Jackson offers no conclusive theory as to *why* this haunting, or any other haunting for that matter, occurs in our world. But we do not need to know. Experiencing the terrors of a haunted place seems to be enough.

This technique of vagueness might drain a story of an immediate accessibility to those readers who prefer their fiction to be steeped in the shiftless reality of daily life, but the strength of this kind of horror story lies in the fact that its reality is akin to nightmare reality, (meaning that the terror is always larger than its contextual appearance).

As a writer of macabre fiction, a number of individuals have been extremely forthright with me regarding the details of their most vivid nightmares. I am not so deluded as to believe that my readers regard me as some sort of dark guru who can interpret the hidden language of these dreams. Rather I think that their candidness is the result of the fact that my tales advertise my willingness to speak of (and indeed *revere*) the unnameable terrors that haunt us during slumber. (However, truth be told, I craft these gruesome little yarns in order to map out my own nightmare country. The fact that you are willing to join me is simply a bonus.)

Another of the nightmare's disturbing qualities is the well-known sensation of ineffectiveness or helplessness that we experience. Whether it is an inability to scream for help or to flee from the pursuer who is drawing ever-nearer with gleaming weapon drawn, we are helpless, lost. It is as if we are merely fodder for some vast dream that does not belong to us and will continue on even after our dream-selves are left butchered in some phantasmal slum.

This sense of ineffectuality and helplessness often lingers after we awaken and re-enter the mundane world. As we sit panting in our darkened bedrooms, watching the familiar sights slipping dutifully back into place, our senses become blunted. Our rational minds are always there to help convince us that the physical world is more tangible than the psychic Hell we've just escaped from, but it nonetheless seems a much smaller, much paler realm of existence. Waking life rarely achieves a nightmare's feverish intensity.

Perhaps it is this raw vitality that makes the nightmare both repulsive and alluring.

There are those of us that hunger for that terrible rush of awe-tinged dread, perhaps to navigate their own nightmare country, to come to understand and appreciate their own cozy niche within the great tomb of sleep.

Such aficionados of the grotesque look for the glimmer of the nightmare wherever they can; savouring its watered-down portrayals in literature, film and other artistic mediums; perhaps hoping that doing so will enable them to master their nightmares.

But no matter how effective art may be, it can never match the sensation of the genuine article. The reason for this is quite simple: in the art-nightmare it is we who are in control. Unlike our own nightmares, artistic horrors can be viewed with detachment. This detachment enables us to analyze, even toy with, the trappings of our Gnostic Nightmares.

Perhaps by probing the art-nightmare we manage to deepen our comprehension of the Gnostic Nightmare. Maybe gorging on fictitious horrors enables us to cultivate a reverence toward the abyss that calls to us in waking life, toys with us in nightmares, and in death ultimately claims us.

—Richard Gavin
Ontario, Canada
Summer, 2006

In the Shadow of the Nodding God

We cannot know how horror began, can never gauge its boundaries. Nor have we any hope of comprehending why certain individuals seek communion with it. I am therefore restricted (as we all are) to conceiving and sharing the details of my own personal role *within* this particular horror; a role that was brief, peripheral and painfully inconclusive.

My role began during a highly tumultuous phase of my life. Long before any supernatural intrusion I had been plagued with numerous anxieties. Some of these anxieties had no basis in physical reality, others did. Because of my condition, I had always felt that my grasp on reality was tenuous at best. Teetering safely back from the cusp of insanity was a constant struggle. I lived in perpetual terror of what I might find waiting for me if I ever were to tumble beyond the brink of reason.

Ironically, it was only after I submitted myself to a maniacal existence within the very heart of horror that I found peace. When dwelling in a womb of blood and brimstone my days became malleable, my nights infinite. And whenever I did emerge from the psychic sanctuary I'd conjured for myself, I found the material world intolerable. Outside my private garden of unearthly delights I was a lost soul, a transient in a world whose rigid laws seemed utterly futile to me.

Sadly, many of the details of my experience are distorted by two irrevocable impurities. The first is the machination of human memory, whose natural tendency is to opiate even our most traumatic experiences until they become nostalgias that we long for in our autumn years. The second impurity is the falsely surrealistic worldview that is brought on by insomnia; a condition that plagued me then; and on occasion does still.

My Season of Damnation (as I like to call it to appease the poetic yearnings of my imagination) began in early summer. That year I had found employment in a plant that manufactured steel fittings. I was never told exactly what type of machinery the fittings were designed to service, but was only instructed by the gruff foreman at the beginning of my first shift that my sole concern was "to make sure that this part," he said, holding up a steel elbow joint, "and this part" (holding up a length of steel tubing) "join together snugly at the seam. Understand?"

And so from dawn until just after noon each day I would be hunched between towers of archaic machinery, studying the same steel fittings that paraded past me on a wobbly conveyer belt. I would mindlessly inspect them, and by my rough calculation approximately one in every thirty fittings was defective. There were undoubtedly more unusable pieces, but I was often too tired or simply too disinterested to be more diligent in my inspection. The job was lonely and mindless, but was not without its advantages; namely the fact that I did not really have to concentrate or speak to anyone for the majority of my shift. Usually the only time I would open my mouth was when the foreman swaggered by to, as he put it: "Make sure things were flowing smooth as milk."

The nature of the job allowed me to spend a great deal of time meditating upon a queer hobby that was born of my insomniac's mind ...

*   *   *

I don't know how I ever came to discover Gideon's; the town's 'purveyor of old paper.' It was most likely during one of my late-night wanderings through the 'Town Square'—a cluster of shops and cafes that was designed to resemble a Victorian marketplace; complete with cobblestone walkways, streetlamps crafted in the style of gaslights, and shops with red-brick facades and hand-carved hanging signs.

Much to the dismay of the Town Square retailers, the average customer seemed to prefer the bright, air-conditioned sanctuary of the nearby mall. This was evident by the fact that of the twenty or so storefronts in the Square, only nine were occupied. The others were coffined-up with sun-faded "Space for Lease" signs; their interiors hollowed of everything but dust and darkness.

Of those few businesses that did manage to stay afloat, Gideon's was the only one that interested me. His shop provided me with many hours of aesthetic indulgence. Its basement-like showroom was crammed with every manner of paper product one could imagine—sepia-toned photographs of nameless people and forgotten places, yellowed newspapers that detailed long-forgotten events, obscure books whose leaves were riddled with silverfish. There were even bundles of handwritten letters which Gideon bound with scarlet ribbon and sold for five dollars per stack.

Stranger than the inventory was the fact that Gideon's never seemed to close. Rarely did I ever encounter another patron inside the shop. Yet no matter what time I stopped in, whether during my lunch-hour or in the thick of pre-dawn darkness, Gideon was always there, apparently waiting for me; always dressed in the same threadbare cardigan sweater and always nursing a mug of strong-smelling black coffee.

After he'd had enough time to study my buying habits, Gideon began to cater to my eccentric tastes. He would often stash an item or two behind the counter for me to examine during my frequent visits. Often these items were little more than hackneyed tabloid confessionals involving extraterrestrial abductions, or were cheap paperbacks that detailed particularly grisly regional crimes, but every so often Gideon would produce a true gem whose morbid glamour suited me perfectly.

I can't imagine that the old man had a more loyal customer than me.

It was only after I had amassed a rather sizeable collection of grim and Fortean literature that my hobby began to evolve into something more than the simple amassing of old paper.

The initial idea had come to me during one of my customary restless nights. It was a veritable revelation. I rummaged about my apartment until I found the old scrapbook I'd been given as a Yuletide gift many years prior. Into this I began to paste the choicest photographs and news clippings from my collection.

Initially these collages were assembled for purely artistic reasons; configuring creased photographs beside strips of newsprint in just the right manner.

It was some time before I realized that what I was actually doing was constructing my own twisted history of this little town. By pasting an arbitrary photograph alongside a totally unrelated news-clipping, I reconstructed reality. (I recall one of my creations; an early favourite which featured a photograph of a cherubic young girl pasted above an unrelated article on a rash of unsolved strangling murders that were taking place in and around the town's harbour district at the turn of the century.)

As with all creative endeavours, my fabricated history books quickly assumed a life of their own. Gideon began to provide me with increasingly stranger material to work with; almost all of which chronicled the grim events of human life, or offered even grimmer speculations about the dim realm that remains hidden from us in the course of our day-to-day existences.

I don't know whether my histories grew stranger because of this new source material, or whether my source material became more deranged to suit my creation, but regardless of the reason, the pages of my scrapbooks quickly began to fill with images of cadavers whose eyes I had replaced with almond-shaped slivers of tinfoil so that their lifeless gaze would have the shimmer of mercury drops. I used very thin razorblades to reconfigure pictures of century-old farmhouses until they resembled Gaudi-esque palaces. I inserted tiny monster faces where their windows would have been; filling their vacant rooms with abominations.

Although it felt very proper, very *right*, to be creating what I was creating, my work eventually led to my suffering severe nightmares during those rare nights when I managed to sleep at all.

None of the actual images or events of these nightmares were perceivable, but their impact certainly was, and my already brief teases of slumber were soon usurped by night terrors. Needless to say, startling awake inside a room filled with ghoulish scrapbooks was anything but a comfort.

By this time my late-night explorations of the town had become a compulsive habit. These treks were not the result of insomnia alone, but were also due to another terrible compulsion I had developed: an insatiable hunger for amphetamines.

I had only looked to narcotics after my nightmares became too much for me to bear. A young man on the factory staff had introduced me to the pills. He earned extra money by peddling various illegal substances to coworkers during lunch-breaks or between shifts. After experimenting with many different drugs, I found that none of his less abrasive opiates were able to erase the dreams, so I resorted to popping four or five of the little egg-shaped amphetamines in order to stave off sleep altogether.

When slumber did become unavoidable, I found that the impact of the night terrors had been dulled. Initially I believed that the drugs were responsible for this, but I now know that it was because I had already begun to embrace the reality of the horror I had unwittingly been perpetuating.

As the weeks wore on, the amphetamines gradually provided me with a decidedly different service. Although I had initially taken them to exorcise my night terrors, I soon required the pills' stimulation in order to stay awake and create more of my scrapbooks—the only thing I cared about.

My customary routine became to steal a short nap upon returning home from my shift at the fitting plant. I would then eat whatever scraps of food I had on hand before venturing out to Gideon's. Later I would return home with a bundle of new material and would then ingest a few amphetamines to sustain me through the moonlit hours, which I spent gleefully cutting and pasting the grotesquery I now so desperately wanted the outer world to conform to.

Looking back, I now realize just how palpable the Presence in my home was. Crouched over a coffee table that was tattooed with blotches of dried glue, tiny wedges of cut paper and mounds of musty newsprint, I would often feel the back of my neck bristle with gooseflesh. And whenever I did peer over my shoulder I fully expected to discover something leering directly behind me, hissing words of encouragement, begging me to take my work deeper into the abyss. Though my eyes never detected anything during those many late nights, my spirit unquestionably did. Little did I know that I would soon witness my visitor as a tangible entity.

This self-destructive existence went on for longer than I care to admit. I constantly questioned myself about why I had allowed my delusions to overtake my life so thoroughly. But it was only after I lost my job at the fitting plant, and my subsequent lack of finances forced me to move into a crumbling boarding house in the most impoverished area of town, that I began to perceive my work in a larger context; a facet of a system that was broader than my own meagre compulsions. I was struck with the feeling that all my efforts were actually *leading* somewhere. It felt as if all the mad chronicles, all the drug-soaked dreams, all the night terrors, were in fact a prelude, an act of preparation, the opening of a door …

*   *   *

My work reached its critical mass during a late-night walk.

Instead of wandering to Gideon's, I impulsively chose to take a more rustic route, one that led me out of the residential district and onto a dirt road that wound its way across the farmland that lay beyond the town limits.

While I wandered past the green fields whose blades hushed and nodded in the night wind, my brain hummed from the effects of the handful of pills I'd gobbled earlier in the evening. Autumn had already reaped the area of much of its lush vegetation, leaving desiccated leaves and a chill as pale replacements.

I was shocked when I suddenly spotted a strange edifice jutting up from the barren land, reaching contortedly to the sky.

A house.

All other details of my surroundings were instantly stilled, muted. The house became the All.

It was situated at the edge of what was once a sprawling cornfield, but was now a wasteland of curled husks and withered shocks. What drew my attention to this structure, the element that made it so eerily compelling, was the fact that it was an exact replica of one of the mutilated homes I had constructed for my history books. It hosted the same towering, needle-thin foundation, the same claw-like design (with its rooms sprouting up in individual turrets like curled fingers), and the same oblique lean, as though the house was a bird of prey looming over the earth.

Entranced by my own disbelief, I found myself wandering in the direction of the outlandish structure. Dead plants crunched beneath my shoes. A small, diabolical core of my imagination throbbed with countless images relating to the house. I allowed these visions to wash over me, caring little that none of them had any basis in reality. Obviously the house was not really composed of primal sludge and brimstone, nor was it built by a legion of arch-daemons. But that was how I envisioned the history of the house, and so, for a brief time, that was its authentic history.

I used this same diabolical imagination to navigate me around the parameter of the structure until I reached the large door, which looked as though it had been fashioned out of hardened mulch. I was not at all surprised to find the door unlocked, nor was I shocked at how inviting the house's interior felt when I finally crossed the threshold and moved into the windowless foyer.

The air was stale, rife with various aromas of decay. I stood in the darkness for a few thoughtful moments before concluding that if I did not explore as much of the house as I could before this hallucination ended, regret would send me to an early grave.

I shuffled forward, groping until my hands closed over the cold firmness of a steel railing. One by one I scaled the cragged steps that ascended through the house in a hysterical spiral pattern. Some of the steps were only a few inches high, while others were so steep they actually required me to use my arms to hoist myself onto them. At the end of my climb I was standing within a large circular room whose walls must have been made entirely of glass, for I could see the sky's vast nightscape churning and glinting all around me.

A crescent moon primed the room in soft illumination, affording me a vague glimpse of the figure that was seated behind a large table at one end of the room.

In the substandard light the figure resembled the simple silhouette of a man. No features were visible other than the basic outline of his slight, motionless body. From my vantage point the figure seemed to be bald, for his cranium appeared to be reflective and was perfectly oval-shaped in the semi-darkness. The same could be said for the area where its face should be, for I could only discern a perfectly smooth surface—a large black egg perched upon a spindly neck.

I took a step forward. The figure raised its hand.

"That's not necessary," it said. The voice was soft and rather androgynous. *"I need only to speak with you. We have been monitoring your efforts for some time now."*

The figure gestured toward the desktop, which I then noticed was littered with a variety of books. The figure flipped one open, apparently at random, tilting its head to the open volume. It then began to nod; a gesture I took to be a sign of approval.

"On the whole we deem your documentation to be exceptional."

"But ...," was the only word I managed.

"But?"

"Fictions," I replied, "they're only fictions."

"Artifice," it hissed, *"the secret definition of beauty."*

The figure tenderly closed the volume. I felt my brow furrowing; a habit of mine that I unconsciously do whenever I am perplexed. I couldn't help but wonder if the books on the desk were actually the ones I'd created. But how could they have gotten out of my apartment, and why? No one but me knew of their existence. No one but me could appreciate their import.

No one that is, except perhaps the entity before me.

"You needn't worry about your documents," it said. Its obscured form moved out from behind the desk. It took three slow steps toward the centre of the room. *"We have taken the liberty of depositing them here; a place where there is no risk of them falling into the wrong hands. It is time that you and I discussed the next phase of the Revealing."*

As the figure drew nearer, a powerful feeling of vertigo began to overtake me. The floor beneath me softened. The light from beyond the windows started to ripple, to fade out, and then to instantly brighten again. In this funhouse illumination the figure appeared to be surrounded by a deep blue glow. This palsied aura rippled off his black body like heat waves, yet the figure cast off no warmth. Not even when it reached its fuming hand toward me ...

I staggered backward, repulsed at the very thought of those grim fingers pressing against my skin. I began to scrabble down the crazy staircase, but when I finally reached the bottom step I found the figure there waiting for me. His form filled the massive doorframe.

Before I collapsed into a slumber of indeterminable length, I heard the figure pronounce:

'*Your reception of the next phase cannot be avoided ...*'

I awoke to find myself slumped upon a mound of smashed bricks and cinderblocks. My body was being lashed by a cold, earthy-smelling wind. My head ached terribly.

I stood up feebly, glancing at the charred hull of an old farmhouse that had clearly been ravaged by a fire many years previously. I stood in the centre of the ruins, looking over the scabby, soot-smeared brickwork. Only a small portion of one wall remained standing.

'The pills,' I told myself as my eyes fell upon the human-looking silhouette that the smoke residue had left upon that last remaining wall. Pills and poor lighting had brought the image to life. Nothing more.

Somehow I managed to carry myself back to town, and to my room, which, as I discovered immediately upon entering, had been burglarized. The thieves had ransacked what few possessions I did own before escaping through a shattered window. I reported the robbery to the police, and submitted to them a list of items that had been stolen. These included my television set, a few CDs, and of course my scrapbooks and all the material I had purchased from Gideon's.

When I asked one of the officers what the odds were of any of my possessions being recovered, she shrugged her shoulders, informing me that the police had "far worse things to work on than this." In one respect her observation was true, yet in another it wasn't.

I visited Gideon's some time after the robbery. He was sympathetic to my case but explained that almost all the items he'd sold me were irreplaceable. Perhaps this is just as well, for I can now live out the rest of my days without any physical reminders of the process which led to my being noticed by a hidden watcher of this world.

And the "next phase" that the shadowed one spoke of? Alas, I am quite certain that you will remain immune from the effects of this prophecy. I believe it is solely my destiny to apprehend this reality; this unfettering of conjured forms, this influx of impossibilities, this *damnation,* is meant for me alone. Whether it was created by me or dealt to me by providence is irrelevant. Yours will remain a sheltered, vibrant world. Mine stays a gaunt and morbid place.

Nightly I can sense the chimeras of my imagination tumbling into the unlit corners of this hovel that houses me. The grotesques of my insomniac dreams have peeled themselves from the brittle paper of scrapbooks to become my sole companions. With them alone do I wander the slums, beneath a sky alight with crooked stars, in a town whose twisting streets lead to nowhere.

—1—

Four years ago, when Rupert first opened New Aeon Books, his intention was to establish a boutique that purveyed only what he deemed to be "meaningful artefacts." Said artefacts consisted mainly of brittle-paged volumes on occultism, tarnished statues of forgotten gods, and the sundry accouterments used in spiritualism.

Much to his dismay, the local network of occultists was too scant and too poorly funded to keep his shop afloat. So, purely for fiscal reasons, Rupert was forced to expand into a more lucrative (and much seedier) niche. Never one to cater to what he called "the suburban worldview," Rupert rejected my suggestion to stock the drooping shelves of his store with mainstream literature, and opted instead to peddle pornography.

At first he assured me that he would keep only a single rack of adult magazines and videotapes behind the counter as a concession to the paying rabble whose income Rupert planned to funnel into his chosen inventory of artefacts. But as the years progressed, Rupert's selection of occultist fare dwindled. New Aeon gradually, almost imperceptibly, metamorphosed into one of the city's largest dealers of rare and fetishist pornography. The shop became so notorious for its collection of outré smut that patrons like me, who still looked to Rupert to provide rare volumes of mysticism and magic, felt ashamed to enter his tiny retail space, which sat at the end of a slumped, time-battered plaza.

Whenever I stepped inside New Aeon I felt a little like those men who babble about how they only purchase adult magazines for the articles. I would have happily acquired my tomes elsewhere if it weren't for the fact that Rupert still demonstrated an uncanny skill at procuring the scarcest occult titles imaginable, often selling them to his friends for a third of their market value. I special-ordered most of my collection over the telephone, putting off venturing to the actual store until my order had arrived.

It was during an otherwise drab Saturday in March that I made a trip to purchase just such an order; in this case it was a rare volume of Theosophical essays that I'd been rather eagerly waiting for.

I pulled the door to New Aeon open and its hanging chimes clanged. The noise dragged the attention of the store's patrons away from their flesh-smeared magazines and onto me. Rupert was standing behind the raised counter, serving a young woman. He glanced up to offer me a slight nod before returning to his customer.

I moved swiftly to the occult section, hoping that the other customers would take note of my lofty interests and perhaps suffer feelings of spiritual inferiority. I slid a volume of Wallis Budge's woefully inaccurate books on Egyptology from the shelf and idly flicked through it while I waited. Periodically I would steal glances of Rupert and the woman with whom he was whispering.

It was evident by Rupert's *sotto voce* that the woman was not here to purchase books on metaphysics. And while it was not unheard of to have female customers purchasing pornography here, I could not recall ever seeing a woman as elegant as the one that presently spoke to Rupert in murmurs.

She was dressed in a long coat of very soft-looking black leather. Two slender boots with very high, very narrow heels poked out from beneath the coat's hem. Her hair possessed the colour and gleam of polished copper. Her facial profile revealed delicate, almost feline features.

Rupert finished looking through the stack of papers. But it was only after I saw him retrieve the cashbox from beneath the counter and place several bills into the woman's gloved hand that I realized she was actually selling, not buying. The woman gave a throaty "thank you" before turning to exit the store.

The chime over the door clanged. She was gone.

I waited until a rather anxious-looking man in a wrinkled suit made a terse, shaky-handed purchase of some videotapes before I finally moved to the counter.

"Good afternoon, Seth," Rupert said to me, dropping the nervous man's money into the cashbox. "Here for your book, I take it?"

"Who was that woman?" I asked quietly.

Rupert sniggered. "You know, for someone who finds all of this material morally repugnant you certainly seem interested in who's reading it."

I shrugged. "I just didn't expect to see someone like her in here, that's all."

Rupert smiled crookedly. He tugged a cigarette from the crushed package that sat next to an overfilled ashtray. "Exactly who *do* you expect to find here?" he asked, half-rhetorically. "If you must know, that woman was Elizabeth Campbell." He paused to exhale blue-grey smoke through his nostrils before adding, "Emerson's daughter."

"Emerson had a daughter?" I asked much-too-loudly. I have never been one who is able to mask feelings of shock or excitation, though any information about Emerson Campbell should not have really shocked me. Aside from being mine and Rupert's spiritual teacher, Emerson was the most secretive man I'd ever known. He had last been seen some eight months ago, but none that knew him thought this at all strange.

Emerson's obsessive nature, coupled with his unconventional interests, often manifested as highly unpredictable behaviour. The only personal detail that I knew about Emerson had emerged from the gossip that was forever circulating through the Paranormal Society, of which Rupert, Emerson and myself were members. The rumour was that Emerson had lost a substantial share of his fortune in a bitter divorce from a woman named Lois. But this was many years ago.

"Evidently," answered Rupert. "I met her after the last Paranormal Society meeting."

"Does she have any idea where Emerson is?"

"She said he's engaged in a rather intensive retreat somewhere in Switzerland. I think he's actually staying in the villa that Lord Byron lived in for a time."

"What for?" I asked.

Rupert shrugged. "That's all she told me. The other day she phoned me to say that her father had given her some items to take back to Canada with her. Items, he told her, that I would be interested in."

Before I could say anything further, Rupert tossed a stack of tattered sepia-toned photographs in front of me. They splayed over the coffee-stained countertop.

My eyes were assaulted by graphic shots of women dressed in corsets or in petticoats, engaging in activities I liked to think did not occur in the more civilized Victorian age. There were clusters of men too, some of whom wore porcelain masks in the shape of exotic beasts. I pushed the photos back toward Rupert, who found amusement in my admittedly priggish reaction.

"I never thought the Steward of the Paranormal Society would keep pictures like that," I said, almost sulkily.

"It seems that old Emerson has more hobbies than phantom raps and ectoplasm," Rupert said. "Victorian porn is quite popular, actually. You often see it reprinted in art books. Admittedly, these shots are a little more graphic than most. But, to each his own."

"And Emerson gave these to his *daughter?*"

"Yes. He said it was important that I see them."

A cold weight of disillusionment began to press down on me. Images of Emerson Campbell flickered past my mind's eye. I thought of the grand old Steward standing at his lectern, dressed in his regal attire, espousing his soul-chilling truths about the hidden universes of mind and spirit. I thought of him this way, and then I thought of him stashing away smut in his sock drawer. The very idea caused my heart to shrivel.

"I really did just come here for my book, Rupert."

Rupert retrieved my Theosophy book from the backroom and we completed our transaction wordlessly. I departed and made my way to a nearby cafe to enjoy a coffee and, with any luck, a renewed sense of Mystery by reading my latest acquisition.

As a man for whom socializing causes untold stress and anguish, I often find myself replaying past interactions over and over in my head. During these episodes, I compulsively reassess what I should have said during a given conversation, or what such-and-such a person was really trying to tell me through the ciphers of so-called casual conversation. The night after my interaction with Rupert, I found myself analyzing our encounter in New Aeon. But it was only after a few days had passed that revelation finally struck. Ordinarily I never act on my imaginary revisions, but my insight into this situation, I felt, merited investigation.

I phoned Rupert during my lunch hour at the Museum of Natural History, where I worked as a curator.

"New Aeon Books," said the low voice on the phone.

"Rupert, I have something to ask you."

"Seth?" he said, exhaling cigarette smoke. For an instant I thought I could actually smell the burning tobacco seeping through the tiny holes in the receiver.

"I know it's none of my business," I began, "but why would Emerson want you to see those pictures? And if they were so important to him, why would he have his daughter sell them to you?"

For many seconds, silence was Rupert's only reply. Then:

"The money was simply to reimburse Emerson. But Seth … this isn't an appropriate discussion for the phone. If you don't have any plans, meet me at O'Bedlam's Pub tonight at nine. We can talk about it then."

Later that night the two of us were nursing pints of bitters inside O'Bedlam's. Rupert was chain-smoking and prattling on about everything but the subject he knew was most pertinent to me.

"So?" I finally blurted out.

"What?" he replied coyly.

"The pictures."

Rupert reached into his jacket and extracted a tattered photograph. I looked about, mortified that someone might see me with the picture. When I glanced back at Rupert, he was holding the photo in front of his chest, in plain view of the pub's other patrons. I reached over and slapped the picture down onto the tabletop.

It depicted a very gaunt man sprawled nude over a chaise that was upholstered in brocade fabric. The man was in a state of high arousal, due to his own manual gratification. In his other hand he held a hookah pipe which snaked its way out from beneath the man's handlebar moustache like a surreal tongue. Smoke wafted around his face, which was a mask of sheer abandon.

I handed the picture back to Rupert.

"I'll never understand your attraction to all of that," I said.

"In time you will."

"I don't see what that picture has to do with what I asked you this afternoon."

"Everything," Rupert replied. "Emerson told me about these pictures years ago. They're his prized possessions. In fact, you might say they are his magnum opus."

"I highly doubt that," I said, feeling the resentment creeping into my voice. "The man is the Steward of an established spiritualist group. Even you can't honestly say that a collection of sex pictures outshines his achievements within the Society."

"No, I'm saying that these pictures are an *extension* of his work in the Society; a culmination of that work, if you will."

"I don't follow."

Rupert paused to light yet another cigarette. "It's a pursuit that Emerson likes to keep quiet about. I doubt anyone other than me is even aware of it."

"Why did Emerson involve you?"

"Probably because he knew I wouldn't judge him. I'm no fool, Seth; I'm keenly aware of my reputation within the Society. *Unsavoury* seems to be one of the more popular adjectives that the other members use to describe me."

I ineptly tried to protest these theories, but Rupert dismissed my excuses with a wave of his hand.

"I'm not ashamed or embittered," he said. "As it turns out, my reputation actually served me quite well. It led to Emerson inviting me into this highly secret area of his work. Not to mention the fact that he set me up with my own business."

"Emerson owns New Aeon?!"

Rupert chortled. "You didn't really think that *I* could ever afford to open a shop, did you?"

I shrugged.

"Please, Seth. I could barely scrape together rent money when Emerson proposed the project to me. Dealing pornographic material was his idea, not mine. And contrary to what I've led you to believe, it wasn't added to New Aeon out of financial necessity. It was Emerson's goal from the very beginning."

"But why did Emerson go through all the trouble of funding a retail operation just to expand his collection?" I asked.

"The collection is incidental. Porn is simply a catalyst for what Emerson is actually seeking."

"Which is?"

"Take another look at this picture," he instructed, "a *close* look."

He pushed the hookah-smoking man back to me. I looked it over as discreetly as possible. Despite the fact that I was trying to be academic in my examination, I could still feel myself blushing.

"Do you see it?" Rupert asked.

It was as if his words somehow guided my eyes to the precise spot in the photograph, for at that moment I saw the "it" Rupert was referring to. I saw it, and I shuddered.

Within the fuming clouds of hookah-smoke there appeared a vague, half-formed silhouette of a woman. The only visible body parts were those that were swathed in smoke. The figure was perceivable by the same principle that makes certain types of jellyfish visible; their otherwise transparent bodies becoming visible when placed in coloured water. In this case it was the smoke that defined the woman's breasts and torso, and the one hand that was pressed against the reclining man's chest. A curtain of long, misty hair obscured the woman's face.

"Trick photography?" I asked.

"Not according to Emerson. In his opinion, *that* is an authentic succubus—one that was inadvertently caught on film by a nineteenth-century pornographer."

"So, Emerson is really just investigating spirit photography?"

"That's just the beginning. Why don't we go back to the shop, Seth?"

The temperature outside had dropped considerably during our stint in O'Bedlam's, so I welcomed the warmth of Rupert's tiny "apartment," which was in reality a small section of New Aeon's storage area behind the showroom. With only a moth-eaten curtain separating the shop from his personal living space, I began to understand why Rupert always seemed self-absorbed and obsessive: his life was a constant meditation on sex and mystery.

A battered steamer trunk was at the foot of the cot upon which I sat. Rupert unlocked the trunk, pried its creaking lid open. I could hear the rustling of papers as he fished out a variety of items. There were further examples of sepia photos, but also slick-paper magazines of modern pornography, as well as a few pulp-era digests.

"These are just a few more examples of Emerson's collection," Rupert explained. He fanned the items out over the fibrous bedspread. "If you look carefully at this photo spread from the 'fifties, and then this one from 1961, you can see the same smoky form in the corner. Now, this magazine, which is from…" he flipped to the cover to confirm the publication date, "September 1988 doesn't have any ghost photography because modern photographers would never allow for any sort of flaw. But, if you look very closely at this model here, you'll notice a very peculiar characteristic."

After some examination of the woman's admittedly alluring body I murmured:

"She has no navel."

"Very perceptive," Rupert replied. I felt an odd tinge of pride from his recognition.

"But what links this woman to the spirit photos?" I asked.

"Emerson is adamant that this woman is the same entity as the woman in the smoke. His theory is that as time wore on, male lusts grew sharper and more ... *colourful,* shall we say. This in turn strengthened the succubus' presence in the material world. In other words—increased exposure to the collective male lust endowed this succubus with a flesh-like body and enabled her to walk among us. It's a lofty theory, but you know how Emerson prattles on. But I do really think he might be on to something."

Rupert moved to switch on a small television set and rather archaic VCR, both of which sat atop a bookcase crammed with fat occult tomes: *Magica Sexualis, Succubi in Medieval Europe, Spectral Rapture and Possession.*

"I want you to see something else," he said. Slipping out of the back room briefly, he returned with an unlabelled videotape, which he plunged into the VCR.

"Don't worry. I won't subject you to the actual movie."

After a few minutes of fast-forwarding and rewinding, Rupert apparently found what he was looking for.

"Now, look closely here."

I did my best to overlook the mass of grunting actors and actresses whose bodies had entwined to form what looked like an otherworldly insect. A blonde actress slinked into frame. Rupert pressed a button on the VCR remote control and suddenly the actors were all copulating in slow motion.

I watched. And then, for a fleeting moment, the succubus appeared in her true form. The blonde woman's carcass seemed to part, to split, and from it there bloomed a cloud of leering fog. Part-arachnid, part-hag; the apparition scuttled about on tendril-like appendages. It skittered over the cluster of actors, all of whom appeared to still be lost in carnal abandon.

Then, a subtle transformation took place amongst them; a transformation whose swiftness allowed it to occur without my noticing. Rupert had to rewind the tape and bluntly point out the fact that the flesh of many of the actors wrinkled once the smoke touched them. Their skin instantly withered, like rotting fruit. One actor's hair was also instantly bleached of its pigment. I watched it turn salt-white in a matter of seconds.

Then, as quickly as it had arrived, the pale thing disappeared. It was once more incarnated in the blonde woman who resumed groping her fellow actors.

I exhaled sharply.

"Can that be the same woman as the one in the pictures?" I asked. "There are so many years between them, and she looks so drastically different in each piece."

Rupert nodded. "I know. But remember what we're seeing isn't her true form. That strange fog is her essence, not the human body that encases it.

"Emerson and I did some digging to track down the director of this film to ask him about the woman," Rupert explained as he mercifully switched off the television. "The director remembered that they shot the movie in an abandoned mansion, which, not surprisingly, had a reputation as being haunted. He thought it would be a good place to shoot a 'blue movie.'"

"Did he say anything about the woman?" I asked.

"No. He didn't remember her. That's the other thing. None of the photographers, directors or actors remembers the woman. She always just appears in photographs or in films; an apparition that perhaps no one actually sees until after the fact.

"Anyway, the director of this particular movie did say that the house they shot in felt very eerie to both him and the cast. He also said that there were a lot of strange happenings during the two-day shoot."

"Such as?"

"A constant sense that he was being watched, sudden banging noises from different parts of the house, and the grandest of all; the director told Emerson that one of the actors, who had been resting in the master bedroom between takes, suddenly ran screaming out of the room and tried to flee out the front door. When they finally did manage to calm him down, the actor said that while he was in the bedroom he'd heard a woman's voice. And before he knew what was happening, the man suddenly awoke as if from a deep sleep to find himself perched on the window ledge, a mere inch or two from a three-storey fall onto the stones below. The voice had somehow talked him into jumping out the window."

I offered a theory that the man could have been suffering from a temporary possession and Rupert agreed. This apparently had been Emerson's theory as well, and that was what had inspired him to undertake a very thorough investigation of the house.

"What did he find there?" I asked.

Rupert shrugged. "I wish I knew. Months went by, and then the next bit of information I got was from Elizabeth telling me that her father was on this Swiss retreat."

Here Rupert's recollections simply ended.

"So that's it?" I blurted in frustration. "We don't know anything further?"

"Not yet," Rupert replied.

"What do you mean?"

Rupert pulled one of occult volumes from the shelf, flipped open the cover to retrieve an airline ticket he'd stashed between the musty pages.

"Emerson has paid for me to join him in Switzerland. Elizabeth gave me this ticket the other day. I'm going by his house on Friday to pick up some documents and a bit of cash from Elizabeth, and then I'm off. I'd ask you to come, but it's a very hush-hush affair. I'm sure you understand."

"Yes, I suppose I do."

"That reminds me, can I borrow your video camera in case Emerson and I need to do any documentary filming of our séance work?"

"Of course," I replied. "But I have to say, I have a bad feeling about this."

Rupert laughed. "That's the curse of the occultist, Seth; we're all so bloody superstitious."

The following morning I returned to New Aeon to deliver my camera to Rupert. It would be the last time I'd ever see him alive.

—3—

Rupert left for his trip and I spent the ensuing four weeks waiting, waiting, forever waiting.

I ventured to New Aeon almost daily, only to find it closed with the same hand-written sign in the window announcing that the store was CLOSED FOR RENOVATION.

I considered contacting Elizabeth Campbell to inquire about Rupert, but decided against it, knowing that Rupert's trip had been confidential.

After a tedious eternity, I finally received a sign.

I would like to say that the sign came in the form of a letter from Rupert informing me that he and Emerson were both alive and happily at play in their spiritual vacuum. Tragically, it was far more ambiguous, and therefore more ominous.

A videotape. It was unlabelled and arrived in a padded envelope with neither a postmark nor a return address, but somehow I knew it was from Rupert. The tape's content was a wordless tour of a Victorian Gothic mansion set deep within a rustic countryside. Although there was nothing immediately familiar in the setting itself, intuition told me that this house was the lair of the spectral harlot.

The camerawork was nauseatingly unsteady, the picture plagued with blurs and glitches and a recurring sheen of static. I could see the wet-looking stone exterior and the gabled windows and the spires that were choked with ivy and kudzu.

The opening moments of the tape consisted of the cameraman (who I felt in my heart to be Rupert) staggering through the brush on their way to the great, shadow-laden house. The crunching of twigs and the sound of laboured breathing were audible on the tape, as was the low, almost lamenting wind. Tiny droplets of rain splattered against the camera's lens, smearing the imagery on my television set. The sight of the rain dribbling down the screen, combined with the wordless panorama of the eerie environment, made it seem as though I was the one approaching those large doors at the rear of the great stone house.

The cameraman's movement momentarily ceased. A hand appeared at the bottom of the screen. I then heard the squeaking of a rusty hinge. The door was lethargically pushed open.

The blackness of the empty mansion swallowed the screen.

At this point I could only assume that the cameraman entered the mansion, for the noise of the rainstorm was suddenly muted and I could hear the echo of footsteps upon a firm marble or stone floor.

I was so intent of scrying out the details of what was happening on the tape that I actually found myself crouching just inches away from my television. I peered into the corners of the screen, as if doing so would reveal some hidden clue that was nestled in the screen's edge.

There was a clicking sound and a shaft of white light abruptly sliced through a portion of the screen's darkness. The sudden introduction of light actually caused me to wince. The cameraman had obviously switched on the camera's spotlight, which he then beamed about the room, offering me brief glimpses of the house's interior.

He appeared to be standing in a great hallway or foyer, for the spotlight revealed an empty wooden coat rack whose spindly metal arms seemed to me to be reaching out hungrily, and a closet piled with dozens of old dirty shoes.

The cameraman gasped with heart-stopping suddenness. Had he heard something? Seen something?

The images on the screen began to wobble; something I attributed to the cameraman's trembling hands. The camera moved through the long foyer, then stopped abruptly. Rustling sounds were audible, and then the image of a single white rose filled the bottom portion of the screen. The flower crept into view, rising up like a queerly-textured moon. Once he had made the flower visible, the cameraman simply held it there. His unsteady hand caused the rose to wobble as though it was caressed by a cold wind from somewhere inside the darkened hall. For several minutes I sat watching the quivering flower, listening to the panicked breathing and what sounded like whimpering. I waited to see if the significance of the flower would be revealed.

I was reaching for the fast-forward button when I heard the shriek.

My remote-control tumbled to the floor. I clearly must have missed some rapid transformation on the video, for the once lush rose had been replaced by a scant bud of browned and brittle petals. I quickly rewound the tape and discovered that the cause of the cameraman's shriek had been the almost instantaneous withering of the white rose in his hand. The petals shrank, faded and fell away in little more than a single heartbeat. It was like viewing a time-lapsed film played at an absurd speed.

A second image followed the decaying rose; one whose effect on me was all-consuming terror.

A woman—so old she was no longer incarnate—glided down the large stairway without the benefit of any of her vaporous limbs. Her head wobbled on the thin neck like a balloon. The face's details were blurred by weepy waves of heat, the kind one sees in a mirage.

The eyes were closed, the nose half-decayed, and the mouth ... *the mouth ...*

It gaped wide and hungrily, like an uncapped sewer.

The face slid closer to the camera.

The cameraman's squeal was abruptly cut-off, as was the imagery on the video. A blizzard of static replaced the visual blasphemy.

I stared at the snowy screen until the cassette reached its end. I reviewed the tape a dozen times that night, but each viewing only caused further bewilderment and deeper dread.

It was clear that I had to get in touch with Elizabeth Campbell. Although this meant that Elizabeth would discover that Rupert had broken his oath of silence, her assistance was now vital. The situation had grown dire.

I searched frantically for Elizabeth, but it ended up being a fruitless, circuitous affair. Clearly the woman had already left the country, perhaps to join her father and Rupert, wherever they may be.

After much frustration I did eventually manage to acquire the telephone number of Lois Vaughn, Emerson's ex-wife of many years, from a somewhat loose-lipped Society member.

Lois Vaughn was understandably aloof during my initial phone call to her. She had never shared her former spouse's passion for the supernatural, (in fact she later admitted to me that she was a staunch materialist), so my Society affiliation with Emerson greatly decreased my chances of arranging a personal meeting with her. But after I poured on an embarrassing dose of charm, Lois agreed to meet with me.

—4—

I was unsure what to expect from our meeting, which took place at her apartment in a nearby suburb. It was evident that the old woman had been looking forward to my visit, for she had gone to the trouble of preparing lunch for two. It was also evident by the handsome furnishings that filled her sizeable apartment that her divorce from Emerson had been as lucrative as the rumour mill had implied.

While we ate, I listened to Lois blather on about all manner of mundane topics while I waited for an opportune time to present my questions concerning Emerson and their daughter. When a lull in the conversation finally opened up I cleared my throat and said: "I was hoping, Ms. Vaughn, that you could assist me in unravelling something of a mystery."

"I'm intrigued," she replied with a warm smile.

"It's about your husband ..."

"*Ex*-husband," she corrected.

"Ah, yes. As I said, it involves him, but also your daughter Elizabeth ..."

The smile drained from her withered face. Her eyes suddenly seemed glassy, cold. Her brow knitted.

"You're mistaken, young man," she muttered.

"I'm sorry?"

"Emerson and I never had children."

The back of my neck suddenly felt very hot. The marzipan cake I had been eating turned bitter on my tongue. I washed it away with a sip of tea, whose flavour was now sickeningly metallic. Was there no circulation in this apartment? Oxygen seemed to be bleeding out through the oak-paneled walls.

"I don't ... I ..." My words were so feeble that I could not even be sure I uttered them aloud.

"No children," she repeated. She clunked her cup and saucer down on the table as an exclamation mark.

While scrabbling for an explanation I further offended my hostess by suggesting that Emerson might have had a daughter with another woman.

"Certainly not!" she spat. "We remained childless because Emerson is physically unable to procreate. The doctors confirmed it shortly after we were married. Now, my young friend, you have overstayed your welcome. Go!"

I left the woman's apartment with a whirl of apologies. I remember little of the journey back to my home.

The following days were a dull-hued blur. Life moved at a crawl for me. I meditated on the succubus, on Rupert, on Emerson, and then the succubus again.

Then, on that fateful night, I decided to pursue one final avenue of investigation. I grilled the same loose-lipped Society member (who, ironically, was the Society's secretary in charge of our membership's most confidential information) over the phone until he finally gave me the directions to Emerson's isolated mansion.

I made the tediously long trek along winding country roads, all the while praying that my aged vehicle would not break down. I was overtired, ill-prepared (I had not even packed a flashlight), and nearly paralyzed with fear.

I arrived at the mansion in the deep hours of the night. The house sat bathed in the blue glow of a gibbous moon. Its doors were locked, its windows shuttered, its gardens and lawns all horribly overgrown.

It looked as aged as the house in the video.

And then I realized that this *was* the house from the video. Emerson's mansion. It had been here all along. Was this what Rupert was trying to convey with the videotape? Or was I lured here by some other force? Perhaps it wasn't him behind the video camera after all.

My heart rate quickened. My throat felt desiccated. It took all my willpower to force myself out of the car and into the night, with its damp mist, its cricket song, its dense shadows.

I roamed the grounds for what must have been an hour, peering through grime-obscured windows and wiggling snug doorknobs. I found no hope of entry.

I was about to leave when I happened to notice that the door at the rear of the house, which had a moment ago been tightly locked, now hung half-open, beckoning me.

As I approached I noted that the overgrown rose bushes that grew on either side of the back entranceway were now withered into brown and brittle husks.

I entered the mansion through the back door. I recall that the house was excruciatingly dark and that I had to feel my way through each room.

Almost manic with fear as well as a morbid curiosity, I explored the rancid-smelling kitchen, the tomb-like sitting room and the seemingly infinite staircase that led to the second of the mansion's four storeys.

My body was soaked with perspiration and my heart felt as though it was about to burst, but the compulsion to persevere led me up the winding stairway until I reached the house's summit.

A tiny trapdoor was the only barrier between me and the Campbell attic. The trapdoor opened with very little pressure.

The attic smelled as though many life-forms had been condemned to die inside its sharply-angled walls. Even though the attic seemed darker than the rest of the house, I somehow found my eyes growing accustomed to its utter lightlessness. This nyctalopic ability enabled me to discern the outline of an enormous bed that stood against the far wall. A bundle of sheets and coverings were piled upon its mattress. The white pillows at the head of the bed seemed to glow like plump clouds in the darkness.

All was silent; so silent that I was able to hear the soft rustling of the bedclothes. I was paralyzed, able to do nothing more than stare as the sheets began to rise from the mattress in a great mound and advance toward me.

One by one the bedclothes slid from the moving shape. They fell to the floor, all twisted in the wake of the shape's movement. What these sheets veiled was an amoeba-like blob of smoke-light, which was soon wholly exposed.

At first the shape seemed to be floating. It cascaded nearer. I smelled a cold, foul scent, like that of rotten flora.

Wispy tendrils of white smoke began to congeal into what looked like bleached flesh. The smoke coagulated further to form a human face, the face of a woman; the woman we'd thought was Elizabeth Campbell.

Nearer she came to me. And, God help me, I wordlessly summoned her to come nearer still.

Her breath was cold and dry against the nape of my neck. I could feel myself trembling. It was so severe that for a moment I felt myself fainting. Her lips moved up to mine; almost touching. Static crackled between our gaping, eager mouths.

I closed my eyes, waiting for her kiss. Waiting for it. Wordlessly pleading for it.

"Eat," I heard myself whisper, *"feed ... "*

What ensued was not a kiss, but sickness. Strength and will vacated me. I waited for her to take me.

Rupert's face suddenly flashed through my mind; hurling the peril of my situation to the forefront of my mind. A deep gushing sound filled my ears, like the roar of circulating blood.

"Stop!" I shouted, "STOP!"

A panic rooted in self-preservation exploded inside me. As this fear grew, my desire ebbed. I staggered backward, my arms flailing in the darkness. The banishment of my lust seemed to infuriate the ghost-whore. I suddenly remembered one of Emerson's teachings about confronting the demonic. He'd told us that they were always forces of chaos; mindlessly hungry. The simplest way to drain their power is to ask,

"What are you?" I asked. "Tell me what you are!"

The vague contours of her body began to fizzle and fade.

"You are not of this place. What are you? Tell me now!"

An inhuman howl then filled the air.

Without any apparent repercussions, the entity was gone.

I felt a sudden gush of frigid air pass over me, and after this, felt nothing at all.

When I next opened my eyes I was slumped on the dust-padded floor of the Campbell attic. I was alone. Murky pre-dawn light was bleeding in. It was the colour of dishwater; a sickly illumination, a hue one might use to describe the pain of migraine headaches.

I pulled myself up from the floor.

As I stood listening to the silence, I thought of how deceptive and cunning preternatural forces can be. Why do we insist on venturing into exotic locales, into sealed tombs and crumbling temples, to seek occult energies? Does darkness not seep into the places so near and familiar to us that we scarcely notice its presence?

This wraith seemed very wise to the fact that lust needs no sacred space; it blooms in the heart of every man, in every city, during every age.

Yet this pale lover—this catalyst for all the dark, incomprehensible passions of men—remains ageless. She stands aloof (one might even say mockingly) from our everyday world. Venturing near only when we are obsessed by Her, at which point She consumes us, claims us for Her own veiled purposes … a purpose She herself may not even fully understand.

I staggered toward the trapdoor, stopping when my foot pressed down on something sickeningly soft and moist.

In knelt to examine what looked to be a pool of congealed fluid. I could not determine what it was, and would have not thought any more of it, had I not spotted the pile of copper-coloured hair that lay just underneath the glistening mass.

I fished out my latchkey from my jacket pocket and used it to poke, and eventually lift, the strange substance.

In the half-light the substance appeared to shimmer like sun-dappled water. It was a pelt, a skin that had been shorn the way a serpent sheds its old hide. I could distinctly see the gaping eyeholes and the mouth that drooped open in the hollowed face. The empty sleeves of arms and legs dangled uselessly at the sides of the gutted torso. My eyes were pulled to where the creature's belly would have been. Of course it bore no navel, for it had not been born of a mortal woman.

Adjacent to the hideous skin there laid a rectangle of glossy paper. Its lurid colouring seemed to glow beneath its coating of dust. It was an airline ticket, unused. Like Emerson, Rupert had staggered unwittingly into the diseased womb of the Pale Lover and had lost himself there.

Delirious, I allowed the skin to slip off the tip of my latchkey. I made my way down the seemingly endless stairs. Sunlight was shining in through the open backdoor. It illuminated the dusty pieces of my smashed video camera that were scattered across the foyer floor. I stepped over the debris and into the waiting morning.

—5—

Getting what one feels is essential out of life can become an obsession, one that requires a shameful amount of deception and fawning. I admit to using every psychological trick I knew in order to coerce Emerson's ex-wife to allow me to take over the duty of running New Aeon Books. "Just until Rupert returns," I told her.

Shutting down the shop would have been much easier for her since the business was one of the many messy details she'd been forced to deal with since Emerson's disappearance.

For the past ten months I have served as New Aeon's proprietor, turning over any financial profits to Lois Vaughn. She in turn allows me to sleep in the back of the store and run the shop as I see fit.

rIcHaRd gAvIn

The only after-effects of my encounter with the Pale Lover (and really the only scrap of evidence I have to convince me that the encounter actually occurred) are a rather severe vitamin deficiency that forces me to take a number of pills and occasional mineral injections, and the fact that my hair is now as white as ghost-smoke. But such trivialities mean nothing to me now.

My vocation involves poring over videotapes and magazines that exalt the worst traits of humanity. The only gratification I draw from this pursuit is the occasional glimpse of a smoky-faced woman, or of a man whose expression of bliss teeters on dread. Anomalies such as these are the only clues I have toward unravelling the truth behind the vanishing of my companions.

I do not know if I will ever unearth the full story, but I take solace in the fact that I am not alone in my quest. My regular clientele also seem to be searching for something equally elusive. The transactions at New Aeon are always brief, for both buyer and seller are too immersed in the passions of half-formed fantasies to be distracted by the dealings of the world of flesh and stone.

Clayton Grant bolted upright in his bed. The congregation of shadows within the room was only faintly disrupted by the late-summer moonlight that leaked in through the stained-glass windows. The lunar rays endowed the painted images of various Saints and martyrs with an ethereal glow. Clayton glanced at the clock that was perched atop a pile of unpacked boxes: 3:09 a.m. He sighed and rubbed his grainy eyes, hoping to push some of the cobwebs from his mind.

Had he even fallen asleep? Surely he must have. Clayton ran through a compressed replay of the evening's events: A drive-through supper from the nearby Burger Palace, then back home to unpack cartons of chinaware and books and small kitchen trinkets. He'd tucked Julia in for the night (all the while trying to ease her fears about her inaugural day at Bishop's Cove Elementary School; an event that now loomed a mere two days in the future). Laura had gone to bed early. Clayton had considered unpacking his canvases to try and to do some painting, but he lacked the motivation. Instead he'd joined Laura in bed where they'd talked a while, fooled around affectionately but listlessly (for both were too exhausted to actually consummate their urges), until Laura finally drifted off at around eleven. Clayton had tried reading a small portion of *The Sundial* by the glow of the small bedside lamp, but little of the text was registering. After that he must have dozed off.

Then … a clanging sound. It jarred him from sleep. Bishop's Cove was a tiny seaside village, so rustic that its houses merely peppered the otherwise sparse landscape around the bluffs, so naturally Clayton had expected an almost eerie silence to permeate his new home, particularly in the wee hours. The tinny ringing that sounded just outside his window was disheartening, and more than a little frightening.

The metallic clang repeated, louder this time. It was a small bell, surely.

Clayton snuck over to the one window whose glass was not stained, but secularly transparent. He hunched below the low ledge, his hands cupping his genitalia like some ridiculous codpiece.

The moon frosted the surrounding lot (whose grass was badly in need of trimming) with a cold shimmer. Clayton craned his head about, listening to the incessant bell. Careful to keep his naked form concealed, Clayton peeked out the bottom corner of the window, his eyes straining to survey the edge of his property. His gaze followed the drooping wire fence that barricaded his lot from the gravel road beyond.

When he caught sight of the figure lumbering along the narrow road, Clayton had to will his muscles to go lax, for he'd been taut to the point of aching. Though the air in the room was warm and still, Clayton's jaw began to tremble, his teeth chattering like a wind-up toy.

The figure on the road moved sluggishly, as though it were measuring each step with compulsive precision. It was too distant for Clayton to see any specific characteristics, but the figure's body appeared slight, and Clayton had the impression that the man (?) was rather old. This was due not only to the figure's snail-like stride, but also to the noticeable stoop. The shape resembled a great question mark as it hobbled down the road; dressed in rags of shadow, a bell swinging noisily in its left hand.

The figure's right arm was extended, clutching something large and dark, something that Clayton could not identify.

There was a small measure of relief for Clayton when the wanderer appeared to walk right past the tiny chapel where Clayton huddled.

But this relief dissolved when Clayton saw the figure abruptly stop and slowly crane its head—featureless in the night—around to face Clayton.

Of course the man was merely looking in the direction of the house, but to Clayton he was glaring directly *at* him, staring *into* him; into the soft curds of his brain, the misty aether of his soul. Clayton threw himself down onto the unswept floor, out of view of the man with the bell. He hunched himself like some timid animal. His heartbeat lent the scene a rapid, pounding soundtrack.

Time passed; two minutes, or perhaps five. Clayton attempted to read the bedside clock but could not, at least not safely. So he waited.

Surely the figure had left by now.

Clayton then heard the squeak of a rusted hinge.

'*The gate,*' he thought.

The crunching of gravel was then heard. It was a carefully measured rhythm. The stranger moved up the path toward the front steps of the chapel. Clayton could then hear the scuffing of soles upon the chipped stone steps.

Laura had left a few of the emptied packing cartons out on the porch earlier in the evening, and the stranger now seemed to be rummaging through them. What could it possibly be looking for? The stranger must have hurled one of the boxes in frustration, for Clayton heard it land with a hollow thud.

'*This is your house,*' Clayton thought, '*your family. Protect them.*'

But he could not. All Clayton could do was squat and tremble and pray that this intrusion would end soon.

The moon was then suddenly eclipsed, its glow blocked by a dark form that was pressing itself firmly against the bedroom window. Clayton could see the vague contours of the figure's hunched shoulders, and his cocked head. He could even hear the soft chinking as the bell's pendulum rolled inside its metal shell. The intruder was on the other side of the glass, mere inches from Clayton. Yet Clayton knew that the man was also somehow not there.

Clayton glanced over at Laura, who had never looked frailer or farther away.

'He sees her ...'

"What do you want?" Clayton cried.

Laura snuffled loudly.

Clayton could see her reaching across the mattress for him. When her hand found only twisted bed sheets, Laura righted herself and immediately called her husband's name.

The moonlight returned with all the swiftness of clouds being cleared away by night winds. Dreamy luminescence flooded back into the room, revealing Clayton in his foolish-looking position beneath the window.

"My God, what's the matter, Clay?" Laura asked.

"Nightmare," Clayton answered almost sulkily. He wiped the slobber from his still-quivering chin before adding, "I must've walked in my sleep."

Outside, the ringing of metal resumed; faint and ghostly in the distance.

*   *   *

"Maybe he used to be pray here," Laura suggested as she dropped two slices of bread into the toaster. "You know, the ghost of some disgruntled Christian invading your heathen dreams to exact his revenge."

"Very funny."

"What's very funny?" Julia asked sleepily. The child stood in the kitchen's doorway, wearing her checkerboard-pattern pyjamas, rubbing her eyes.

"Daddy's dream last night," Laura replied, "and good morning to you too, young missy."

"Did you sleep well?" Clayton asked as his daughter shuffled into the bright kitchen.

"Not really. What happened in your dream, daddy?"

Clayton blew on his coffee, eyeing Laura through the curls of steam that wavered before his face. She shrugged, smiling.

"It was just a silly dream, Julia," Clayton said flatly. "What would you like for breakfast?"

"I'm afraid you're stuck with peanut butter on toast," Laura interjected. "I'll try and get to the grocery store this afternoon. Come to think of it, where *is* the grocery store in this town, Clay?"

"There isn't one. The closest things are the farmer's market that runs out of the schoolyard, but that's only on summer Sundays. You could try the General Store out on Cove Road."

"That's all?!" Julia huffed.

"I didn't realize supermarkets were so important to a nine year-old," Clayton said. "Don't worry, there's a Red-and-White supermarket just outside of town. You and your mom can take the car and go there."

"Do you have any painting to do?" Laura asked. Her tone was ambiguous.

Clayton was unsure if she wanted him to say yes so that she knew he would be happily occupied, or to say no so that he could help her unpack.

"I'm not doing any painting until we get through some more of these boxes," he replied.

He leaned toward the kitchen window. Two or three slabs of cardboard littered the overgrown lawn. The gate at the end of the gravel walkway hung half-open like a broken jaw. Clayton willed himself not to shudder as he rose from his chair.

"Where are you going?"

"I want to clean up the yard before I start unpacking. Some animals got into the trash last night."

He kissed Laura's cheek, he ruffled Julia's hair, and then he exited the kitchen.

The morning was cool, but Clayton could feel the promise of heat in the air. This afternoon would most likely be uncomfortably humid. He traipsed across the lawn, dew soaking through his deck shoes. He collected the collapsed boxes and re-latched the gate. Erasing the evidence of last night's occurrence was done with ease, for Clayton had managed to steel his mind against any memories of the clanging bell, the shadow on the path, the shape at his window ...

He found the note as he was righting the overturned recycling bin. The paper had been stuffed between the corroded curlicues of the porch's iron railing. He slid the sheet free. Its bond was thick, more akin to parchment than wood-pulp. Uncrumpling the sheet, Clayton read:

> *'Remember the clocks,*
> *Look well to your locks,*
> *Fire and your light,*
> *And God give you good night.*
> *For you the bell ringeth darkly.'*

The penmanship was flawless. It appeared to have been laboured over, crafted with a care that bordered on fanaticism. The evident care of the note made Clayton strangely envious of its author. He thought of how striking his paintings could be if he himself could adopt such discipline.

The arched door of the chapel groaned. Clayton turned to see Julia emerging to greet the morning. Although only a few moments ago she had been shuffling, zombie-like, in her pyjamas, his daughter was now dressed in brightly coloured shorts and a T-shirt, her chestnut hair tied back in a ponytail. She bounced out into the waiting day; a psychedelic star shooting out from the otherwise dim interior of the sanctuary.

"Where are you off to?" Clayton asked.

"To play," Julia replied. "Mom said I could."

"What about the grocery store?"

"We're not leaving until mom's cleaned the bathroom. I'll be back in time. What's that, a letter?"

Clayton let his hand fall. He nonchalantly concealed the paper behind his back. "No," he said, "just some litter. Stay away from the bluffs while you're playing. And don't roam too far, OK?"

"OK."

Clayton watched his daughter trot off toward the gate. The shrill squeak of her prying it open was the midwife that birthed the image of his visitor skulking its way back into Clayton's imagination.

Clayton watched Julia shrink along the pathway that wound from the chapel and into the nearby woods. Although the sky was virtually cloudless, the air felt strangely damp and charged with ions, as though a storm was gathering nearby. Clayton chalked this sensation up to sleep deprivation and resumed cleaning.

Every inch that Clayton cleaned seemed to reveal more work: The wire fence would have to be torn out and replaced. The gravel lot was riddled with potholes, weeds and other people's trash. And this was to say nothing of the chapel itself; with its flaking rust-coloured paint, its ancient wiring, its curling roof shingles.

Clayton's mind drifted back to Laura's initial reaction to the property. *'Pretty,'* she'd said, *'but even with the cheap price we'll end up spending a king's ransom on renovations and repairs.'*

Clayton had been motivated by his artistic temperament more than he cared to admit. To live in a rural chapel, to have a nave decorated with his own paintings, to work without disruption; such things were worth any price. Life seemed to have been dragging him away from his innate creativity; replacing it with Sunday dinners with the in-laws, parent-teacher meetings and Julia's dance recitals.

But now that he had committed not only himself but also his wife and child to what he believed to be his chosen lifestyle, Clayton was beginning to feel that moving into the old chapel was a colossal mistake. An acrid taste filled his mouth. His belly was beginning to ache.

Better not to meditate on these things.

The day had grown noticeably brighter. Through the open window Clayton could hear the sound of Laura scouring the tub; an attempt to bring order to at least one portion of their new abode.

"Daddy?"

It was more of a whimper than a voice, a flute-like ripple of sound.

Clayton spun around to see Julia standing behind him. Her face was the colour of salt. Tears rimmed her eyes. Her tiny hands were trembling.

"Daddy," she repeated, "I found something …"

Clayton bent down to console her, but before he even knew what was happening, Julia had taken his hand in hers and had begun to lead him along the winding path that snaked its way into the woods. Clayton followed her for a while before finally scooping her up in his arms. He planted quick kisses on her cheeks and begged her to tell him what was wrong.

As if on cue, Julia squirmed free of her father's grip and raced over to a patch of grass at the cusp of the bluffs. The drop was sheer, and since he could see nothing but blue sky it seemed to Clayton that he and Julia had reached the edge of the world.

A man-made edifice lined the bluffs' rim. Part wall, part altar; the mass of misshapen stones appeared to have been laid in a horribly complex pattern. Clayton noted the strange glyph-like carvings that had been hammered into the standing stones. Graven images of crude staring faces, of squiggly characters, of strange sigils.

His gaze then moved to the oak tree where Julia stood.

"He's up there," Julia said, her finger jutting up to the leafy boughs. The air was filled with a sizzling sound as a damp wind rolled in off the water and shook the abundant foliage.

Julia referring to her find as "he" shot a shudder down Clayton's spine. His torso felt as though it had been hollowed. He moved closer to his daughter, not truly wanting to see her discovery.

The skeleton that dangled from one of the higher branches appeared to be intact. Clayton estimated its size to be roughly three-feet long, from the top of its malformed head (whose hollowed eye-sockets seemed to be studying Clayton) to the tips of its gnarled feet. Clayton could understand how his daughter would have thought the bones to be human, if one imagined how the remains would look to a child's eyes. It had to have been an animal. But crooked and disproportioned as the skeleton was, Clayton could not deny that in life the creature looked to have been bipedal. It was an observation that made him ill.

"Don't touch it!" Clayton spat, wincing at the harshness in his voice. Julia was still visibly unnerved. She stood trembling. The plump whiteness of her legs was marred by ugly red scratches, some of which seeped fresh blood. Clayton pulled Julia to him, kissed her scalp. Her head was hot, her hair jewelled with perspiration.

"Come on, love," he whispered. "Daddy has to make a phone call."

*   *   *

It was only after he had carried Julia back through the humid fields to reach the chapel that Clayton remembered their telephone was not yet in operation.

"They're coming to set the phone line up on Tuesday, remember?" Laura said as she pried Julia from her husband's arms. "What is it, Clayton? What's the matter? You're scaring the hell out of me."

Clayton rubbed his mouth with the back of his hand, leaving a salty residue on his lips.

"Just keep her inside the house. I'm going to drive over to the General Store and use their payphone." He ducked out of the main room briefly to retrieve his wallet and keys from the mound of boxes beside his and Laura's bed. "I'll explain everything when I get back."

As anxious as he was, Clayton drove at a moderate speed, knowing that to tear along the gravel roadways would only draw negative attention from the other residents of Bishop's Cove, most of who were now out tending to various chores in their yards. He silently questioned why it was he felt the need to maintain the peaceful quiet of the morning.

He reached the General Store in less than five minutes. A stout man dressed in fibrous grey clothing stood sweeping dust and maple keys off the store's front steps. He stopped working long enough to watch Clayton's car glide into the gravel lot.

"Is there a payphone inside?" Clayton asked as he climbed the front steps, mindful not to walk where the man had already swept. For a moment the shopkeeper chose not to reply, and when he did it was only to nod his head once.

"There some sort of trouble?" the shopkeeper asked. His voice was throaty, tainted with a strange accent; one that had less to do with a specific geographic region and more with living many years at a sluggish rural pace.

"As a matter of fact there is," Clayton replied. "I need to get in touch with the sheriff."

The shopkeeper made a sound that could have been a chortle. "Sheriff of where exactly?" He propped his broom against the railing.

"Of Bishop's Cove."

"No sheriff in this town. There's only the county Constable."

"How can I reach him then?"

"You can try telephoning him, but he's probably fishing out back of his house. Your best bet is to drive on over there."

Clayton held back some of his desperation long enough to get directions to the Constable's house.

As he turned to leave, a glitter tugged at Clayton's peripheral vision. A large stainless steel bowl sat at the base of the General Store steps. It was nestled amongst the sprouts of crabgrass like an upturned tortoise shell. Flies buzzed around the small pool of darkish fluid that lined the bottom of the dish. A sheet of heavy-bond paper fluttered beneath the bowl like a trapped bird desperate to take flight. One corner curled up in the morning breeze. Clayton could see that words had been written on the paper's underside with the same night-dark ink; words that were no doubt crafted by the same meticulous hand.

Unthinkingly, he reached for the paper, but the shopkeeper swooped in to retrieve both it and the bowl that weighted it down. As the bowl passed beneath Clayton his nostrils caught a whiff of the fluid's coppery stench. He looked back at the shopkeeper who now dearly held the bowl and the note close to his rotund belly. The man's face had grown ugly with mistrust. Clayton went to his car and drove on.

The Constable's cottage would have been difficult to spot had it not been painted a garish canary-yellow. This carnival hue made the structure visible from the roadway. But only after Clayton had parked his car on the narrow road and begun to approach the house did he realize just how deeply-set into the woods the cottage actually was. It was shouldered by large cedars and veiled by the tangled tendrils of two enormous weeping willows.

Behind the cottage there was a small beach strip, whose sugar-white sands laid flush with the cove. Diamonds of light sparkled upon the water like a constellation of fallen stars.

Clayton stepped onto the cottage porch. The web-work of flora seemed to hold in the hot, sodden air like a lidded cauldron. Clayton found it difficult to catch his breath. He knocked on the door, waited, but met no greeter. His mind flashed with the image of Julia and Laura back at the house, which only increased his anxiety.

Clayton glanced down and noticed a small wooden dish resting upon the lip of the porch.

Of course underneath the bowl was a sheet of paper, its corners rippling from the tiny breeze that managed to seep in through the dense vegetation.

Clayton looked about to assure himself that he was quite alone. Carefully, he slid the paper out from the underneath the bowl, which he could now see held several small bones. Chicken bones; or so Clayton hoped.

He turned the paper over and read:

> *'Through gesture wise*
> *you left nature's prize.*
> *'round this house, peace ring be paced,*
> *Here be felt the Bellman's grace.*
> *For you the bell ringeth kindly.'*

"You need something, friend?" said a drawling voice. Clayton whirled around to see a rugged-looking man dressed in Wellingtons, denim trousers, a faded blue T-shirt. The man balanced a fishing pole and small tackle box in one of his thick fists, and a chain of impaled trout in the other.

The realization that he was standing on another man's property (a lawman's property no less), rifling through his possessions, leapt to the forefront of Clayton's mind. His attempt to return the paper to its proper place was halted.

"I believe that belongs to me," the man said, reaching for the note.

Clayton passed it to him.

"Sorry," he said, "but I found something similar on my porch this morning."

The man looked quizzically at Clayton.

"Where are you from?"

"Toronto. But now I live here."

The man's expression morphed into a slightly friendlier one.

"Are you the fella that moved his family into the old chapel?"

For some reason the constable's question sent a wave of relief through Clayton.

"Yes," he gushed. "My name's Clayton Grant. I'm looking for the county Constable."

"I'm Constable Thomas," the man said. "What seems to be the problem?"

"My daughter found something in a tree near the bluffs. I think you need to have a look at them."

"A look at what exactly?"

"Bones."

"What kind of bones?"

"Not like any I've ever seen."

Clayton thought he saw Constable Thomas' face turn pale. The man looked away from Clayton. He stared down at the ground as though he would find an answer in the soil.

"Give me a few minutes," said Constable Thomas. "I'll meet you at the bluffs."

*   *   *

Clayton made a quick detour to the chapel to check on Julia and Laura. He found Julia happily rifling through boxes of her mother's knick-knacks. Crumpled newspaper, which had been used as padding during the move, had been yanked from the boxes and was scattered over the floorboards like shed skins.

Laura had evidently been unable to occupy herself with busywork. She paced the kitchen floor, chewing her fingernails. When she spotted Clayton she threw her arms around him.

"What on Earth is happening? Julia said she found a dead body."

"Not exactly," Clayton said. "She found some bones over near the bluffs. More than likely they're just animal remains, but I'm going there now to meet up with the county Constable just in case."

Laura wore a mask of shock.

"I'll be back as soon as I can. Please don't get worked up, OK?"

Clayton slipped out of the chapel, pretending not to hear his wife's questions, or her protests.

Constable Thomas was already at the bluffs and must have been for some time, for he had already managed to locate the bones and was busy disentangling them from the tree branches and depositing them into a large clear plastic bag. He was standing on one of the chiselled stones for added height.

"Any idea what it is?" Clayton asked breathlessly.

"Could be any number of things, but to my eye it's a bear cub."

"With only two legs?" Clayton protested. "And look at the shape of the skull."

"The other two legs could've been taken by scavenging animals," rebutted the Constable. "The skull ... well, the cub could have been born malformed. Animals aren't that much different than people in that respect. Now, I'd better be off to make arrangements to have these taken to the city for testing."

"Why bother if they're only bear cub bones?"

"Because I like to be thorough, Mr. Grant" the constable replied as he snapped off the latex gloves he'd been wearing. "You called me out here, remember? I'm just following through. It's my job." The constable turned to begin his departure.

"Wait," Clayton said, grabbing the Constable's bicep. "The bones are only part of it."

Constable Thomas studied Clayton's gripping hand with noticeable disdain. "What else is there?"

"Well, I'm not sure how to put it without sounding paranoid, but there was a man on my property last night. A stranger, he looked like a tramp."

"What was he doing?"

"Snooping around, I guess."

The constable held his stoic expression.

"You know," Clayton explained, "rifling through my trash and things like that. At one point I found him staring into my bedroom window."

Constable Thomas removed the fisherman's cap he'd been wearing. It had left a red ring on his waxy, hairless forehead. "How exactly do you figure that one has anything to do with the other?" he asked.

"I'm not sure. It's just a feeling I have."

Constable Thomas wiped away the beads of perspiration that dangled from his eyebrows. "This person that was sniffing 'round your house," he said, seemingly to no one in particular, "you don't have any idea what he looked like?"

"No, it was too dark."

"It might've been someone from the village who was walking past and decided to make sure that nobody had broken into the chapel. The building's been standing up there empty for a bunch of years now. I doubt many people even knew the chapel was for sale. They were probably surprised to see the boards off the windows."

Thin as the Constable's theory was, Clayton couldn't deny that it *was* plausible.

"Well whoever it was left a calling card; a note, almost exactly like the one I found on your porch, Constable. Do you mind telling me what that could mean?"

"What did the note say?"

"It was a poem, just like yours, or almost like it. Something about the Bellman."

Constable Thomas said nothing.

"Who is he?" Clayton asked.

"Campfire stuff, I guess you'd say," the Constable said with a shrug.

"I don't follow."

"Just a little local colour, you know. Everyone around here was brought up to respect him. He's been around for a lot longer than any of us have, and he'll still be around even after you and I are dust.

"My gramma used to call him 'the Great Protector.' And that's about the only thing I know about him."

"Protector of what?"

"Us. Everyone in the town. It's just a little custom we do. His bell is supposed to keep the air pure. He wards away the far-off things, the things that don't belong here. He takes the gifts we leave for him as payment. That's the Bellman's way."

"So, you're telling me that a ghost left those notes for us? A ghost went through my trash last night? A ghost was at my window?"

"No, not a ghost. This is just a custom we have here, that's all. It's just our way of keeping the peace. You probably heard something about the Bellman from someone around town and had a nightmare about it, that's all. But you'd probably do better to just play along and leave him a little gift each night."

"Custom or not, nobody has the right to go snooping around private property. Or to leave threatening notes."

"Threatening?" Clayton found Constable Thomas' surprise to be unnervingly sincere.

"Would you like to see it?" Clayton said, hearing the anger creeping into his voice. "Now, I don't want anybody coming around my property, Constable. Is that so hard to understand?"

"No," the constable said, his voice soft with what Clayton took to be embarrassment, "no it's not. I best get these bones to the lab in Bolton before they close up for the day."

Constable Thomas started down the path back toward his vehicle. He did not offer Clayton a backward glance.

Clayton stood until the Constable had disappeared, not knowing what else to do. He thought of the bones and of the Bellman. All around him the trees shivered. Clayton allowed himself to do the same before he returned to the chapel.

*   *   *

The remainder of the day was spent on mundane tasks. It took Clayton a few moments to calm Laura's fears about the bones, but she eventually put the ordeal out of her mind. Julia seemed to have done the same, hours earlier.

The three of them went grocery shopping, selecting the makings for a cold supper. The temperature had reached a sweltering high and neither Laura nor Clayton fancied labouring over a hot stove. They picnicked in the lot behind the chapel, nibbling listlessly on ham sandwiches and fresh peaches.

At dusk the temperature began to plummet. They packed up their dishes and went indoors. Laura and Julia began washing the dinner dishes while Clayton continued unpacking.

Laura and Julia both instructed him where they wished to have the television set up in the heart of the chapel. Where pews once sat in tidy rows, the cozy chaos of a painter's workroom was erected. Saints and martyrs frozen in stained-glass were now obscured by towering bookcases, which Clayton and Laura then filled with the many books they'd accumulated over the years (their most sanctimonious title being *The Outsider* by Camus.)

Julia was in bed by nine, and the soft rumble of her snoring could be heard by half-past. Laura and Clayton finished putting the books away and then arranged the living room furniture. They made hurried but still passionate love on the sofa and then sat for a time, listening to the silence before Laura announced she was going to bed. Clayton told her he wanted to paint for a while.

Once Laura switched off the bedside lamp in the small room (formerly the pastor's office, now Clayton and Laura's bedroom), Clayton dropped the charade of mixing oils on his pallet and went about his true task of the night. He slipped into the kitchen and retrieved a length of heavy copper pipe he'd found stashed under the sink.

Clayton sat down at the kitchen table. He thought of reading to make the hours slip by unnoticed, but he knew that doing so would only make him sleepy. So he sat, and waited.

Waited.

The locals could leave little treats if they wished, but he was not about to play along. This was his house now. Not the town's, not God's, not the Bellman's. *His.*

The Bellman came 'round shortly after one.

Clayton could hear it; the tinny clang of a well-used bell. Faint at first; a mere tinkle amidst the chirping crickets and the rustle of the leaves. But the sound gradually bloated to the point where it hurt Clayton's ears. Could Laura and Julia not hear it?

Clayton rose and tried to move as stealthily as possible.

Beyond the cavernous hull of the chapel, Clayton could hear the squeaking of the old gate being pulled open. He quickly crouched down, turned his gaze to the main door of the chapel, listening acutely.

The crunching of gravel came, as did the scuffling sound as of someone lethargically scaling the front steps.

Clayton sucked in his breath. He tightened his grip on the length of pipe and then tore across the nave of the chapel. An instant later he was flicking back the deadbolt lock. With the pipe raised and ready to be swung, Clayton flung the door open.

"HEY!"

It was the only word that jumped into his brain, and he felt stupid shouting it as he leapt out onto the vacant porch. All around him the night seemed horribly still and silent, as though the whole of nature was holding its breath in anticipation of some terrible fate that was about to unfurl.

The porch felt cold as a headstone beneath Clayton's bare feet. The wind gave him gooseflesh.

He jumped off the porch. The gravel on the walkway dug into his feet as he ran around the side of the building, his eyes darting all around him.

The chapel looked forebodingly dark as Clayton ran wildly across its back lot. The Bellman was nowhere to be seen.

Clayton spotted the paper as soon as he rounded the corner of the chapel. He was certain that it hadn't been there earlier.

Tugging it free from the railing, Clayton examined both sides of the paper. It was blank.

Something then dragged Clayton's gaze up from the sheet of virginal parchment, into the still-open door of the chapel. What followed was a strain on his heart. A great cavity began to stretch open inside him. Walking became an act that required great willpower. He moved up the steps, peeking into the chapel, not really wanting to see what might be there waiting for him.

What greeted him was emptiness. Clayton entered the building and the shadows studied him as he moved timidly to his child's room at the back of the chapel. Peering around the partition that afforded his daughter a small measure of privacy, Clayton's eyes fell upon the vacant bed. The sheets were bundled upon the mattress like old rags. The bed was still warm where Julia had, mere moments ago, been lying. The smell of her skin hung in the air. But the child was gone.

The dim room seemed to dilate, to shrink, and then to dilate once more. Alternating waves of chills and heat washed over Clayton as he stared dumbly at the bed; not truly believing what he was seeing.

Laura rushed into the room. Perhaps mother's intuition had woken her, pushing her into her child's room. Perhaps Clayton had unwittingly called for her, or had unknowingly cried out in pain and disbelief. Laura was now beside him, pulling her sheer robe over her shoulders.

"Where is she? Clayton, where's our little girl?"

Laura's face was like a gibbous moon floating in the dark. Clayton stormed past his wife, gasping, saliva shooting through his gnashed teeth.

He tore through the chapel like a man possessed. He raced into the night, not knowing where to run to. Fog creamed the grasses and ringed the trees of the forest. The atmosphere was once again alive with the gentle sounds that are indigenous to the night—the chirping of crickets, the sizzling of wind-kissed foliage, the croaking of toads.

Above all of these elements was the shrill and distant clanging of a bell.

Clayton stumbled toward the bluffs, hoping that the site where Julia had found the bones might lead him to the Bellman. But there was nothing. He crawled up onto the standing stones. He screamed Julia's name like an invocation into the night. He shouted until his throat was hoarse. He searched the woods until the darkness began to cower from the encroaching dawn.

*   *   *

"But you didn't actually see this man up close?" Constable Thomas asked before stealing a sip of the coffee Laura had prepared. He was standing in the Grant's kitchen. Laura was leaning against the tiny counter, her arms wrapped around herself—a pitiful form of self-consolation. Clayton was seated at the kitchen table staring at the mug of coffee that was cooling before him. He did not even think to drink it.

"No," Clayton replied with a sigh of frustration. "I've told you four times now. I did not, repeat *not* actually see the Bellman."

"The Bellman?" Laura snapped. "You mean the man from your dream?"

Clayton muttered, "Not now Laura."

Constable Thomas frowned.

Three officers from a neighbouring county had joined Constable Thomas in the preliminary investigation of Julia's vanishing. Clayton could hear their lumbering footfalls and their warbled voices as they made a ham-handed investigation of Julia's room at the back of the chapel.

There were a number of other questions posed to Clayton by the lawmen, and vice-versa. Neither route of inquiry led to satisfactory results. Finally the Constable announced that he would organize a search party to begin combing the woods, and that he would be back to collect Clayton and Laura for the search later in the afternoon.

Laura broke down just as the officers were preparing to leave. She was slumped on Julia's bed, clutching one of her stuffed toys. Clayton knew he should go to her, but he also knew that there were certain truths that must be found out if anything positive was to come out of this nightmare.

He joined the Constable on the porch and asked him plainly:

"Has the Bellman ever taken a child?"

The Constable hung his head; a gesture that was either pitying or regretful, Clayton could not tell which.

"It's always been give-and-take with the Bellman," he said. "We leave our gifts and he keeps the wolves outside the door. I remember my gramma telling me stories that *her* gramma told her; stories about disappearances during the night; mostly livestock. But there was one legend about a family that lived here in pioneer times; the whole lot of them just up and vanished one night. But those are just some old yarns we all cut our teeth on. I never knew of anything like this happening in my lifetime ..." The Constable's voice trailed off, and when he next spoke his words were firm with reason. "We'll do everything we can for you, Clayton. And if it's any consolation, I am sorry that things played out this way for you. I really am."

*   *   *

Later in the day a search party of thirty-eight volunteers, including a total of nine lawmen, swept the woods. They scoured the bluffs. They dragged the waters. They knocked on every door, searched every root cellar, un-lidded every bin, every dumpster.

Julia was nowhere to be found.

The night fell much too swiftly for Clayton's liking. Eventually the party disbanded, agreeing to resume the search at dawn.

As he and Laura walked back to the chapel, Clayton began to wonder for the first time in his life exactly how much horror the human spirit could withstand. What was his threshold? How much tragedy could he bear before he finally tumbled off the precipice and into utter delirium?

The two of them shared a bottle of white wine in the kitchen. Laura cried until exhaustion and alcohol dragged her into an unwanted but much-needed sleep. Clayton whispered consoling words to her, about how the search would pick up first thing in the morning and that they would never give up until they found Julia.

But as he sat in the darkness at the edge of their bed, listening to Laura's drunken, sleepy babbling about how the Devil had stolen her baby, Clayton knew he would resume the search well before then.

He moved to the kitchen, took up the bottle of wine and emptied it of its dregs. He made sure to sit out of view of the windows.

He once more waited for the Bellman.

The night crawled by. And after a long and silent time had passed, Clayton felt the cold weight of dread sinking in. Perhaps the Bellman had gotten what he'd wanted. Perhaps he would never return.

But, after a purgatorial wait, there came the familiar shuffling sound upon the gravel road beyond, and with it the shrill clanging of the bell.

The Bellman seemed to once more be heading toward the woods. But tonight he did not stop at the chapel in search of an offering. Julia had undoubtedly been more than enough of an offering to protect Clayton and Laura from what Constable Thomas had called "the far-off things."

When he heard the Bellman's footsteps fading into the distance, Clayton burst out of the kitchen. He raced out of in a manic pursuit of the shadowy form that lumbered only a few paces ahead of him.

The Bellman held something in his dark, spindly arms; something that squirmed and whimpered.

Clayton ran with a fury he never knew he possessed. He tore over divots and chunks of stone. Yet no matter now ferociously Clayton moved he seemed to gain no ground on the Bellman. The figure's silhouette maintained its well-measured pace. In fact, the shape did not even offer a backward glance to note Clayton's pursuit. Each time Clayton reached for the Bellman his hands grabbed only air.

Suddenly Clayton was struck with the chilling notion that *he* was the one being pursued. Despite the fact his foe was clearly ahead of him, Clayton nevertheless felt that there was *something* close at his heels.

He could almost hear the following footsteps drawing nearer, nearer …

But there was no time for mental trickery, no time for anything but the chase.

Onward Clayton ran. By now he could hear the waves crashing against the base of the bluffs. He knew the edge couldn't be too far. The fog thickened, or so it seemed to Clayton. Cold curls swayed lazily all around him. The Bellman was now scarcely visible in the mist. He was little more than an ink smear, a vague impression, against a backdrop of fog and night.

The flirtation between moon and mist was clearly capable of astounding feats. For what else could explain the way the Bellman's silhouette seemed to glide effortlessly off the altar stones and begin to ascend in a smooth arc toward oblivion?

"NO!" Clayton cried. His feet scrabbled back from the precipice. Lumps of earth broke away from the lip of the bluffs and tumbled down to splatter against the stones below. "JULIA!" Clayton reached up and began to wrench out clumps of his hair as a gesture of furious impotence. His teeth tore pockets into the flesh of his cheeks. His tongue was soon coated with the coppery flavour of blood. "JULIA!"

All seemed lost.

But then, as if in response to Clayton's pleas, a tiny shadow began to emerge from the fog above Clayton's head. It lunged, frantically grasping at the branches of a nearby tree. The form was small, child-like. Julia had managed to free herself from the Bellman's grasp.

Clayton did not know how he could convey his overwhelming sense of joy and disbelief, so the sound he emitted was akin to a howl. Elation made Clayton's reach into the fog-bearded branches very clumsy.

He knew something was improper the instant his fingers pressed against the cold torso of the approaching form. The skin was clammy, cold, more like wet rubber than flesh.

'He wards away the far-off things ...'

The climbing thing leaned its head out into moonlight. Clayton saw the warped ring of a mouth and the eyes that resembled tiny red plastic beads. A hand—or something like it—reached down.

In that final, fatal moment Clayton realized that the great protector's bell had ceased ringing.

Watery snowflakes splattered against the window, dribbled down the pane like tears. According to the wall calendar today was Christmas Day, but to Thayer White it was merely Tuesday. He stood before a sink brimming with foamy water and too many dirty dishes. The clock above the oven range read 5:51. Without, night was seeping into the tree-sliced skyline of the nearby Four-Points Conservation Area. Thayer still had difficulty referring to the sprawling woodland as anything other than The Cedars; which is what all the locals had called the area for as far back as Clayton could remember. To this day The Cedars remained a popular play area for the local children; and an even more popular location for adults whose predilections were better left hidden in the shadows.

Thayer peered out at the backyard. The fact that the lawn wasn't blanketed in snow but was actually April-soggy weighed heavily on him.

He sighed harshly before resuming the scrubbing of the Christmas dinner dishes.

Strains of Handel's *Messiah* ebbed and flowed from the dining room stereo where Constance, Thayer's younger sister, stripped the oak table of its linen. Her shoes clacked against the tile floor as she entered the kitchen to add a half-empty gravy boat and a platter (which was piled with repulsive-looking chunks of greasy turkey), to her brother's workload.

"Did you bring the empty cartons up from the basement yet?" Constance asked.

"I was planning on doing that in the morning," Thayer replied.

"Well, we need to get the decorations off the tree as soon as possible. The needles are already starting to brown. I don't know why I always buy my tree so early every year, but if we leave it up much longer it will be a fire hazard."

"Uh-huh."

Constance studied her brother's troubled reflection in the kitchen window. She moved to him.

"What's the matter? You've been in a bit of a funk ever since you got off the train."

"I'm just a little tired, that's all."

"Well, Bob and Carol are on their way over for drinks, so I hope you're not going to turn in and leave me to fend for myself."

"Wouldn't dream of it," Thayer said flatly.

"I'll get a fire going in the living room. Would you mind putting a fresh pot of coffee on while you're in here?"

Thayer nodded, but his sister had already click-clacked out of the room. He rummaged through the cupboards until he found the grounds and the paper filters. Once the coffee began to percolate, Thayer wandered into the living room where he found Constance kneeling before the fireplace, assembling a mound of kindling and wads of newspaper inside the mouth of the redbrick hearth. Once she'd used the last of the old newspapers, Constance reached for the copy of yesterday's paper, which Thayer had left draped over the arm of the sofa.

This particular anaemic edition of the 'Pinewood Gazette' bore a headline that was much grimmer than one would expect in a small town tattler:

REMAINS UNEARTHED IN FOUR-POINTS

Constance went to crumple up the morbid front-page. Thayer reached for her arm.

"Um, I was ... reading that," Thayer said apologetically. He released her wrist from his too-tight grasp. Constance replaced the 'Gazette' onto the sofa.

Thayer stared at the headline's bold letters, which were so dark they looked as though they had been sliced out of black leather. The typeface began to blur, to wobble and weep. Abstract symbols began to usurp the words. The sight of them made Thayer's eyes ache, his heart shrivel.

This half-hallucination was curtly disrupted by a great explosion of sound.

The great booming noise was simultaneously thunderous and shrill. For an instant Thayer thought his sister's house was under attack. The noise was like a cannon blast followed immediately with a tinkling sound, not unlike wind-chimes. Constance heard it too, for she allowed the long match she'd been using to light the kindling to tumble from her fingers. It landed in the thick carpet, kissing the grey fibres with flame, causing smoke and stench and brief panic. Constance flipped the edge of the carpet over the blooming fire, snuffing it.

"Car accident?" Constance asked, still kneeling by the patch of singed carpet. Thayer moved to the front window.

Through the lazily swirling mists and the rain and the darkness Thayer could see the vague silhouette of a car crumpled against a roadside cedar. The vehicle had been tossed from the road like a discarded tin can.

Though he could not be certain, Thayer thought he could also see the driver slumped, mannequin-like, inside the cab.

"Call 911," Thayer muttered as he snatched his overcoat from the hall tree. Constance called out to him. Her brother did not answer.

The raindrops were plump and cold. They saturated the fibres of Thayer's wool overcoat as he trudged across the lawn, which was itself a muddy soup.

The car was a compact Volkswagon. Peering into the passenger window, Thayer was able to determine that the driver was a young male. Black fluid was streaming down the contours of the man's bleached face. It took several seconds for Thayer's mind to register the fact that the fluid was obviously blood.

Thayer attempted to pull the passenger door open, but it was locked. Feeling foolish, he nonetheless rapped on the window. Was he expecting the driver to lean his broken body over to unlock the door?

He hurried to the opposite side of the car, only to discover it had been wedged hopelessly against one of the looming trees that lined the desolate roadway. The car was trapped on the border of The Cedars.

He glanced fleetingly at the windshield (its shatter-pattern looking very much like cobweb that splayed very prettily across the glass) and knew immediately that attempting to pull the driver free was too dangerous. He decided to remain by the car until the paramedics arrived. The driver was unconscious but Thayer spoke to him nonetheless, offering even-toned confirmations that help would be arriving shortly; though Thayer doubted this given that it was Christmas Day, to say nothing of the remoteness of their location. As he stood shivering, Thayer's gaze was repeatedly drawn to the mound of cheerily-wrapped gifts that were scattered across the back hatch of the Volkswagon.

"I called for help," Thayer said loudly. His statement didn't seem to be directed to the man in the vehicle so much as it was meant for the night-black labyrinth of The Cedars.

Half an hour later, flashing lights emerged from a dip in the road. Their blue and red illumination looked weepy against the rain. The ambulance slowed once the driver spotted the rain-drenched man waving at them from the side of the road. A local police cruiser soon followed, and, eventually, a tow-truck. Thayer gave the authorities what little information he had; all the while watching as they pried the thin man free from his smashed vehicle. The man was laid upon a stretcher and whisked off in the ambulance. The few snippets of dialogue Thayer overheard between the two medics led him to believe that the young man's injuries were hardly life-threatening.

As the tow-man began hitching up the remnants of the Volkswagon Thayer returned to the house where he found Constance standing in the living room, wringing her hands impulsively. She looked rather grotesque bathed in the multicoloured lights of the Christmas tree. Her eyes were wide and wet.

"Is he ..." she gasped, unable to finish her query.

"He'll be fine," Thayer muttered. "I'm going to take a hot shower before I catch pneumonia."

"I'll try and get a hold of Carol and Bob to tell them not to bother coming over. Chances are they are already on their way over though. I just thank God it wasn't them out there against that tree."

Thayer went upstairs and peeled the sopping clothing from his gaunt body, draping the garments over an empty towel rack in the bathroom.

He took an extremely hot shower, after which he planned to go to bed. But when he stepped out of the steam-lush bathroom Thayer heard voices from the main floor of the house. One of the voices was Constance. He could only assume by the casual tone of the conversation that the other two must be Carol and Bob.

"Thayer?" Constance called from the living room. "Could you come down when you're through?"

He reluctantly threw on a dry outfit and made his way downstairs.

The first words Thayer heard upon crossing the threshold into the living room were: "It's as if the whole town is coming apart at the seams."

The man who uttered this rather ominous phrase was seated upon the sofa. He appeared to be extraordinarily tall with a torso that was almost comically pear-shaped. The woman sitting next to him was not nearly as tall, nor as plump around the middle. Her oval face was embedded with a pair of sparkling blue eyes. Both the man and woman had noticeably greying hair. The man offered Thayer an awkward smile.

"This is Bob and Carol Bookman," Constance announced. "I'd like you two to meet my brother Thayer. He's come home for the holidays."

They exchanged pleasantries. Constance disappeared into the kitchen briefly to prepare their coffees. Once the four of them had settled into their sitting stations in the living room Constance insisted that Thayer relay the details of the car accident, which he did, albeit reluctantly. The middle-aged couple listened intently.

"Well, Carol and I also had a rather grim evening," Bob began once it was evident that Thayer's tale was over. "It just came over the car radio that *more* bodies were discovered last night in the Cedars. Something like eight skeletons, wasn't that right, Carol?"

"Eight, yes," confirmed Carol. "Apparently the authorities unearthed them in the ruins of an old shack back there." The hand gesture she made toward the living room window enforced just how near the morbid discovery actually was. Had Thayer not already been seated, he surely would have collapsed, for all the strength bled from his legs like flowing water. He even reached an unsteady hand to clutch at the chair's overstuffed arm.

He was grateful when Bob decided to change the evening's mood by handing out the gifts he and Carol had brought. Thayer had not been expecting anything, but received a bottle of scotch. The fact that he had nothing to give in return would have made him feel awkward had his mind not been so preoccupied with the images of earth-encrusted bones being culled from the bowels of a weather-bullied cabin deep in The Cedars.

A little after midnight Thayer announced that he was turning in. He bade the guests Merry Christmas and shuffled up the darkened stairway.

Once inside the spare bedroom, Thayer opened the bottle of scotch and stole a few hearty swigs; savouring the burn as the fluid gushed down to his stomach. He flung himself onto the bed and stared at the shuttered window. Moonlight leaked in through the narrow slats, endowing portions of the room with slices of unsettling illumination while keeping others swathed in darkness. The watercolour painting of lilies that hung on one wall seemed to twist into half-visible monstrosities. The clumps of dust that fluttered along the floorboards seemed eerily arachnid. Even Thayer's own hands looked ghoulishly blue in the lunar light; cadaverous, as dead as the boys in the Cedars.

Another mouthful of scotch, then ... sleep.

It must have been a dream. How else could Thayer have found himself wandering the muddy paths of the Cedars in his pyjamas? He could see his breath gushing out in plumes of frost, yet he did not feel cold. A gibbous moon hung bright and full; like a baleful, omniscient eye. It lent the woods an almost midday level of illumination. This made Thayer's journey easier, even though he had no real idea as to the purpose of it.

Gradually, inexorably, Thayer came upon the ruins of the shack.

Yellow police tape had been lashed over the entrance and wound around the surrounding trees. It framed the property like a museum showpiece.

Thayer ducked under the first band of tape and tore the rest from the empty doorframe.

The interior was mercilessly dark. A stench like that of soured milk seemed to cloister within the wormwood walls. Thayer crossed the threshold, only to become suddenly entangled in a mass of what felt like cobwebs. Strands as delicate as cotton candy stretched over his face, tickled the inside of his mouth, clung unyieldingly to his pyjamas and his flesh.

Thayer then saw the old man. Dead, yet still animated, the man was digging, just as Thayer had seen him doing all those years ago. But this time the man employed no shovel—his own fleshless fingers were the only tools he used to claw at the soil floor of his cabin. The man bore crude pockets into the dirt. And into these he dumped the fresh remains of impossibly tiny creatures, many of which were still twitching. It was so similar to the actual scene that Thayer had stumbled upon in childhood.

But in this vision, this mnemonic-dream, the remnants that the old man was burying were not human. And more importantly, Thayer somehow knew that this time he would not remain unseen. This time around he would not be spared.

Once the bones were covered with damp-smelling soil, the old man lifted his half-face to Thayer and pressed a finger of cloud-white bone to where his lips had been. Because the man's head was little more than a skull with a few random tufts of flesh, the old man seemed to be grinning.

Now Thayer could feel the webs tightening around him, pressing into the meat of his body. His head lightened. Breathing became arduous. The webs actually emitted a soft creaking sound as they grew taut.

Panicked, Thayer tore at the tethers. That's when he saw the little makeshift graves beginning to erupt; soil pulsing up and down like earthen hearts.

The things that emerged from the ground were without number. They skittered about with an arachnid's grace. One by one the creatures emerged. And one by one they raced toward Thayer ...

... who immediately shot upright in his bed. The rudimentary sights of the room fell swiftly into place, but brought little relief. The clock on the bedside table informed him that it was not quite six a.m. As Thayer sat, his chest heaving with panicked breaths, a flurry of newspaper headlines, both old and recent, raced past his mind's eye. The black-inked names of his vanished childhood classmates seared his mind, as did the grisly photographs of the recent discovery in The Cedars. Thayer shook the image off, gasping the word, "No!"

Accepting the impossibility of sleep, Thayer flung back the sheets and fished his robe out from the wad of clothing in his suitcase.

The window in the upper hallway exposed an embryonic dawn. Snow was tumbling down like dislodged stars, and must have been for some time during the night, for the ground was now quilted in white. Thayer crept downstairs to prepare a cup of tea.

Standing in the living room, he had to strain to keep his gaze from trailing off to The Cedars; now pure and pristine beneath the snow.

He drank his tea too quickly, feeling his tongue blister from the scalding fluid. Eager to keep his mind occupied, Thayer decided that now was as good a time as any to begin packing up the Christmas decorations, which Constance had requested him to do.

He made his way to the basement to retrieve the battered cardboard boxes that had been used to store the decorations since he and his sister were children.

The temperature in the basement felt a good twenty degrees colder than the main floor of the house. Thayer could actually see his breath flowing out of his mouth in wisps, as it had in his dream. He reached the bottom of the stairs and surveyed the shrine of memories that towered on all sides of him, in dust-laden boxes, in splitting grocery bags, in lidded plastic bins.

A frigid draught grazed Thayer's face. He turned to discover that a jagged hole had been punched through one of the cellar windows. The pane was at ground level, facing the winding street. It appeared that the glass had been kicked in by vandals. The hole was too small for anyone to enter, so robbery was not a possibility. This appeared to have been done solely for the sake of causing damage. Thayer felt the shards crunching beneath his slippers as he moved toward the shattered window.

"Respect," he muttered as he shuffled upstairs to collect a dustpan and whisk, two trash bags and a roll of masking tape. He swept up the remnants of the window into one of the trash bags and then taped the second bag across the hole. The pane would have to be replaced later, for now the plastic shielding would suffice.

He turned his attention back to his original task.

The boxes for the Christmas decorations were piled underneath the cellar stairs. Thayer had to crouch down to fit inside the obliquely-angled inlet. The zigzagging underside of the stairs made the cramped space seem smaller still. He found himself having to breathe just a little deeper in order to keep a level head as he gathered the first of the boxes.

He wrapped his hand around the box, and something cold and moist oozed between his fingers. For a moment Thayer felt as though he'd been de-boned. His body instantaneously lost its strength, so repulsive was his tactile discovery. The box fell to the floor with a hollow thud, vomiting out brightly-coloured tissue paper and plastic trays used for storing glass ornaments.

Stretching from one side of the fallen box all the way to the wall were several strands of a gummy grey sludge. The strands reminded Thayer of pumpkin innards both in appearance and texture. The strands wobbled from the ripples of winter air that still crept in through the poorly-covered window.

The only logical thing Thayer could bring himself to believe was that this was some strange form of mildew that grown in an unkempt corner of the damp cellar. He carefully removed two more boxes, exposing more webbing. He removed three more cartons.

Now the webbing was fully exposed. Thayer was sickened by the sight of it. It was a frenzied entanglement of dripping threads which formed no perceivable pattern, just a crazed intersection of vein-like strands.

And a sulphurous stench.

Thayer grabbed the first thing he could find (an empty watering can) and bashed at the hideous growth.

The mass slipped from the cellar wall from the first stroke. It landed with a sickening plop. Thayer lowered the can again. Something popped under the impact.

Spiders erupted, lava-like, from their smashed nest. Most of the creatures were no larger than Thayer's fingernail, but there were a few whose size caused Thayer to scream. Their bodies were plump, composed of what looked to be some kind of clear jelly. They scurried this way and that. Thayer could not even guess at their number. The watering can cracked into several useless shards. Thayer reached a trembling hand out to grab the nearest box, which he then used to swat the spiders again and again. The box began to crumple from the assault. Fluid seeped into its pulpy fibres, softening each blow. Thayer continued to swing until his pyjamas clung to his sweat-drenched body. Eventually he found solace in the belief that he'd gotten most of them.

The tingling sensation of tiny legs crawling beneath his pyjamas plagued him as he cleaned up the repulsive leavings inside the crawlspace. Every now and again he would suddenly shudder and swat at his clothing, convinced that the tiny monsters were burrowing into his skin.

He plucked the last garbage bag from the package and attempted to bag the mess without having to touch it. He lugged the trash up the stairs, praying that the plastic would not split along the way. Relief came only after Thayer had deposited the bag into the can outside the backdoor.

He shut the door and turned to enter the kitchen. Constance was standing in the doorway.

Thayer was so shocked by her silhouette that he let out an embarrassingly shrill cry.

She was dressed in her bathrobe. Wisps of her greying hair sprung out from her scalp. Her eyes were squinted.

"What are you doing?" she rasped.

"Just tossing out some rubbish I found in the cellar."

Constance yawned, "Well, since I'm up I might as well start breakfast."

"Don't trouble yourself," Thayer snapped, "go on back to bed. I was just going to go for a walk. I'll poach some eggs for us when I get back."

"But you'll freeze out there."

"Not to worry. I have the scarf and gloves you gave me for Christmas, remember?"

Constance gave a feeble smile, her eyelids still heavy from slumber.

"I'll wake you when I return."

The two of them went their separate ways; Constance to her bedroom, Thayer to the washroom, where he scrubbed his hands raw. Beneath the synthetic lavender perfume of the soap he could still detect the acrid stench from the spider's nest.

It was considerably colder outside than he'd originally thought. For a while Thayer simply wandered; pantomiming the actions of a care-free man out for a stroll. But he had a destination, a destiny. Perhaps he went through this charade to mask his burning desire to run full-force toward the ruined shack deep in The Cedars, if for no other reason than to prove to himself that last night's dream was but harmless phantasmagoria.

When Thayer did finally reach the location, it was apparent that he was not alone in his desire to see the grisly landmark. A small cluster of locals had already congregated on the place. They stood behind the yellow police tape, gazing longingly at the recently-turned soil that was being guarded by two uniformed policemen. Bouquets of flowers wrapped in frosted, brittle plastic had been laid along the path. There were also letters and large pieces of Bristol board bearing commemorative poems.

Thayer stepped closer to the police tape; the only thing that barricaded Thayer from the site of so many dark, distant memories. He was lost in the visions now; dreams reifying with the waking world, the ghostly past waltzing with the vibrant present.

"Step back!"

The voice jarred Thayer. One of the officers was walking toward him from the cabin.

"Step back! NOW!"

In his reverie Thayer must have wandered nearer and nearer to the cabin, for the yellow tape had snapped. He glanced up to see the entrance to the cabin a mere two feet from him.

An internal whisper informed Thayer that nothing stays buried indefinitely.

"STOP!" Thayer shouted, not in response to the policeman, but only to the ghosts chattering inside his skull. The officer's expression turned sour.

A spark of recognition flickered in the officer's eyes.

"Didn't I respond to a call from you last night?" he asked. He flicked through the ink-scrawled pages of his notebook, until he found Thayer's name and address.

"Home," Thayer muttered. "Have to get home now …"

The officer scrutinized Thayer's every awkward step as he made his way out of The Cedars.

Thayer's heart felt as though it were about to burst. The winter morning air seemed to freeze inside his lungs.

Constance's house finally came into view. He emerged from The Cedars and made his way to the backdoor.

Entering the house and locking the back door snugly provided only mild relief, for an acrid smell was even stronger within the house, or perhaps it was simply that the scent had leaked up from Thayer's olfactory memory bank.

To add further stress to the situation, the telephone was ringing. Constance was somewhat of a technophobe, hence the rotary-dial telephone in the kitchen and the lack of an answering machine. Whoever was calling was definitely insistent, for the phone rang and rang, even after Thayer had called out to Constance to answer it.

When she didn't, Thayer stomped into the kitchen, leaving wet, evidential footprints in his wake. He yanked the receiver from the cradle just to stop the incessant noise.

"Yes, is this 24 Cedar Lane?" asked a hoarse male voice. Thayer confirmed that it was and curtly asked what the call was regarding.

"My name is Paul Winter. I'm the one who crashed his car in front of your house last night," the man explained.

"Oh," was Thayer's only response.

Unasked, Paul Winter informed Thayer that he had only suffered a mild concussion during the accident and would be dismissed from St. Mary's Hospital by this evening.

"Well I'm happy to hear that you're well," Thayer said, "now, if you don't mind I'm rather busy ..."

"I understand, yes. I got your name from the officer who questioned me about the accident. I took the initiative of finding your phone number and calling you for two reasons. The first was to thank you for calling the ambulance. The second was, well ... I'm not sure where to begin."

"I'm sorry?" said Thayer.

"I ... I saw something last night."

Paul's words intensified the acrid smell to such a degree that Thayer had to brace himself against the kitchen wall to keep himself from crumpling to the floor.

"It must have been an animal of some kind. It came tearing out from the trees. I caught it in my headlights and the sight of it startled me so much that I veered off the road. I feel a bit foolish telling you this, but the thing ... the creature ... it looked like a big hairless spider. There were several legs and a sort of egg-shaped body. I only caught a glimpse of it before I crashed. The police thought I might have been drunk or high, but I told them that I saw a small animal. I'm telling you the truth because, well, the creature scuttled off the road like a shot *and went straight toward your house ...* "

Paul continued to speak, but by then Thayer had stopped listening. Something had pulled his focus away from the telephone and over to the cellar door, which Thayer now realized was half-open.

Thayer let the receiver drop. It dangled, smacking against the kitchen wall, Paul's miniature voice calling out "Hello?" from its speaker. Thayer moved toward the cellar, noting for the first time that there were gummy strands dangling from the jamb.

He was perched at the top of the stairwell. He smelled the rotten smell. He felt the cold, stale air. He emitted a sound not unlike a grunt.

"Constance?" Thayer's foolish query echoed through the unfeeling dark of the cellar. Wet pulsing noises were faintly audible from somewhere below.

Thayer reached for the light-switch. Soggy webbing met his trembling fingers. He pulled his hand back as though it had been scalded.

The trash bag must have fallen from the cellar window. What else could explain the band of sunlight that illuminated a narrow portion of the cellar? Thayer hadn't noticed the light until just now, and when his eyes fell upon the webbing he began to laugh. What to feel, he wondered? What to feel? Dread, revulsion, awe, any of these would have been preferable to the idiotic laughter that erupted from some cracked corner of his soul. But Thayer couldn't stop himself, not even when his gaze panned over to the hand that quivered within the webs.

Thayer recognized Constance's slender fingers, despite the fact that two of them had been picked clean of their meat. He staggered down a few of the stairs, feeling the cold webs lashing against him like tendrils.

The flimsy railing groaned when Thayer leaned against it. A second later it splintered and Thayer tumbled headlong into the webs.

'I am dreaming,' Thayer thought to himself, though this notion did little to comfort him once he heard the webs creaking under the weight of arachnid legs.

The creatures, as large as mature hounds, skittered out from the dim recesses. They were soon upon him, feeding with a ferocity that bordered on delight.

I was depositing my wife's severed head into the soil beneath my basement floor when I heard the telephone ring.

The sound of it chilled my insides. I suddenly felt as though the basement was swaying like a storm-tossed ship. Claire's head was still in my hands; wrapped in old paint rags, bound with thick twine. Her head had a surprising heft to it. Dark fluid had begun to seep through the fibres of the wrapping. I hate to admit that I was actually a little proud of myself for not dropping the dripping package when the phone rang.

The ringing persisted. Part of me thought of racing upstairs to answer it, but the answering machine clicked on before I could take the first step. A dozen names ran through my mind as to who could've called. It might've been one of Claire's co-workers checking in on her, or perhaps my supervisor phoning to see if I planned on calling in sick tomorrow too. Maybe it was someone looking for …

*   *   *

"… Daniel? Daniel? We have to go now." My son was still in the womb of a deep, almost unbreakable slumber. It took every ounce of willpower I had (which was little) to hold back the panic that was trying its best to overtake me. "We have to leave the house now. Come on, son. Wakey-wakey."

Daniel didn't hear me. He stirred once, slightly.

The caller had been Claire's father. He'd left a message, something about how he'd found some jewellery that had belonged to Claire's mother (now deceased) and would it be all right if he dropped the heirlooms by for Claire later today? Perhaps he could stay for coffee?

"Claire's in bed with the flu," I'd told him when I frantically called him back. Talking on the phone was the last thing I'd wanted, particularly to my father-in-law, but I knew that Gordon was the kind of man that wouldn't wait for an answer. Being a widower had eradicated all his social graces.

'Claire doesn't have anything serious, I hope,' Gordon had said. I told him no, babbled a few false promises about having him over for dinner soon, and then hung up.

By then Claire's remains had been fully interred beneath the basement floor. I'd smashed up the cement floor with a pickaxe, and kept Claire's body chilled in the freezer while I dug at the soil beneath. Time prevented me from going as deeply as I wanted, so I ended up dumping Claire's poorly mummified remains into a hole that was only about three-feet deep. I heaved soil on top of the remains, poured out a layer of batter-like concrete, and hastily smoothed the area with a small trowel.

When I stood up to survey my work, it was sickeningly apparent just what I had done down here. It didn't matter. Daniel and I would be long gone before anyone's suspicions led to them disinterring any mutilated proof.

*   *   *

When I was a boy I dubbed it 'Hellbrain.'

I don't know when I first developed this affliction, though I vividly recall the first time that it left me.

Hellbrain feels exactly as you think it would: chaotic and agonizing. It starts with a dizzy feeling, like something living is convulsing at the base of your skull. (Whenever I felt the Earth starting to spin wildly on its axis, I knew an attack was coming on.) Then comes the burning; a fiery pain that I don't have the words to describe to you. It *sears* you. It burns so deeply you can actually see the glow, like fresh-cut rubies, like embers, like sin.

Hellbrain makes the world turn poppy-flower red. Everything you see, every thought that wisps through your mind, scorches you.

And there's a buzzing in your ears, like a chorus of cicadas shrilling within the cave of your skull.

Over the years I learned various techniques for making Hellbrain ebb to a more tolerable level: cold compresses; dark rooms; silence; and pills of course: Ritalin at first, then Zyprexa, lithium, Thioridazine. But even the most potent antipsychotic prescriptions could not erase Hellbrain completely. In the end there was but a single thing—one lone act—that would accomplish this.

I always knew when there was no choice but to unleash my Hellbrain, when I couldn't help but to bore its fire out of my head. In those moments it felt as if nature was working in concert with the Hellbrain, because just when I was at my breaking point with the pain and the confusion, when I was willing to do absolutely anything to make it stop, something warm and vital and living would cross my path; teasing me with the promise of relief.

It didn't matter what it was; a stray cat, a nest of birds, another human being. All that mattered was that they were living, breathing; that they were warm and vital. Plant life never seemed to appease my Hellbrain. It seemed to be drawn to the flesh, to blood.

When you're trapped in the Hellbrain, anything living appeared like cool stream to one dying of thirst. The cicada blast would begin to soften, the agony to ebb. Against the burning red that slathered the world, living things would appear cool and soft. Their very presence promised relief.

My first kill was my sister's tabby cat. I crushed its skull between my bare palms. I pulled at its torso until it tore in two. I yanked out its organs. I squeezed its tiny heart until it popped. It was the single most rewarding experience of my life. Ridiculous as it sounds, I wasn't actually trying to hurt the poor animal. I was only ripping to reach relief, *relief.*

Violence is the tranquil eye in Hellbrain's tempest.

I don't know why it has to be this way. But the compulsion to shed blood, to splay flesh and smash bone is the *only* temporary relief for Hellbrain. (And even its effects are fleeting.) When in the throes of the slaughter, your whole world becomes dappled with a cool soft blue. I've always imagined this glow to be very cool to the touch, soothing. It's tragic that bloodshed is the price of this serenity.

As much as I wanted peace, I tried several times in my life to resist it.

The first time I refused to kill resulted in my having a seizure. I bit-off half my tongue, gouged some flesh from my own face; dripping chunks landed around me like fallout. Fortunately my brother came home early that afternoon, caught one glimpse of me and phoned 911. I was confined to the hospital for months, both for somatic healing and for a long but ultimately fruitless psychiatric examination.

The doctors could never know. I knew, of course; knew that my affliction forced me to commit violent acts, and that Hellbrain was a very apt name for this condition, for who but a Devil would perpetuate such a thing?

Hellbrain affected me from the age of five until the age of eighteen. During that time I found peace by exterminating hundreds of squirrels, cats, mice, and, in my early teens, a total of eleven human beings.

*   *   *

Daniel and I had been on the road for several hours. I asked him if he was hungry and Daniel growled something that might've been an affirmative response. I smiled.

We stopped at the nearest restaurant; a pancake house that sat hidden behind a large filling station and souvenir shop. I could feel the eyes of the others patrons studying Daniel as the hostess escorted us to our booth. Daniel's large brown eyes are always deeply focused on things the average person could never see. He wiggled his fingers in a tight fisted wave, again and again. They resembled squirming grubs. Daniel tiptoed across the carpeted floor. Each step caused tiny red lights to flash on the heels of his Velcro-strap runners. This feature is what had first attracted Daniel to the shoes. The red flashes are minute flickers of Hellbrain. I believe Daniel knows this too. The soles of these shoes are worn to almost nothing; the tops are splayed and perforated, but Daniel refuses to wear anything else.

We slid into the booth and the waitress handed me a menu. She went to do the same to Daniel, hesitated, and then offered the children's menu to me with a phoney smile of sympathy.

"He *can* read," I muttered with disdain.

The waitress nodded once, still smiling. She offered to get Daniel some crayons so that he could scribble over the cartoon characters that decorated his paper place-mat.

It was almost one in the afternoon. I ordered breakfast for Daniel and a beer for me (the very idea of eating made me nauseous). I instructed the waitress to serve Daniel's pancakes with absolutely nothing else on the plate.

"But they come with bacon or a fruit cup," she replied. There was irritation in her voice, as if I was being purposely stubborn and illogical.

"Just the pancakes," I said. "He won't eat if there's anything else on the plate."

The waitress cocked her head to one side; a gesture that revealed her 'I'm-glad-he-isn't-mine' attitude.

I stared out the window while we waited. My stomach went cold every time a car pulled into the parking lot. Daniel ran his pinky finger along the dizzying circle of lines that formed the maze game on his place-mat. His hair was spiky with uncombed tufts. I could see the faint beginnings of a moustache begin to sprout beneath his freckled nose.

The waitress finally emerged from the kitchen area and I could see the fruit cup sitting on Daniel's plate. She stopped halfway to our table to remove the fruit cup before bringing us our food.

*   *   *

To this day I wish it had been me who'd kept the Hellbrain. By college I had pretty much learned to control it, or at least make it bearable. Pain management was essential for me back then, for the Hellbrain had become an incessant anguish. Sometimes it would be milder than others, but the agony never went away completely.

That is, not until that one afternoon with Claire. We were at her old apartment on Freemont Street. It was a cramped, narrow space with warped floors and a water-damaged ceiling. It was springtime; a mild day. I remember smelling the rich fragrance of various budding flora that came creeping in through Claire's open bedroom window. My head was aching quite badly that day, but Claire was feeling unusually amorous, so I did my best to forget about the pain while I began to kiss her, to undress her, to guide her back onto the creaky futon.

As we made love the pain inside my skull mushroomed. Russet-coloured amoebas splattered in my peripheral vision. Bile squirted onto my tongue. Claire knew I was in pain and did all she could to aid me. She rolled me onto my back. She asked me if I wanted her to stop. I told her I didn't.

56

We both came simultaneously. Claire moaned with delight. I cried out in agony, because the instant before my orgasm my pain reached a new zenith. It paralyzed me. I felt as though my insides were being squeezed with hot wire. But then, the instant my orgasm passed, my Hellbrain dissipated. It didn't shrink to a dull ache, it didn't wane; it vanished. One second it held me at its mercy, the next ... gone.

I began to laugh. Shock had made me giddy. Claire couldn't figure out why I was laughing, and I didn't bother to explain. I held her. And we talked for a little while. She eventually drifted off.

I nuzzled Claire's sleeping form against me while my mind raced with questions. I refused to accept that whatever was responsible for the Hellbrain would simply alleviate it for no reason. Why?

And then the answer dawned on me, and it levelled me completely: Claire was now pregnant. I knew, somehow I just knew.

I'd tried to act delighted when she phoned me from her doctor's office two months later. I managed to feign excitement when we moved into our first apartment together.

I was in the delivery room the night Daniel came into the world. I even snipped his sinewy umbilical cord while he squawked and swatted at the air with his tiny limbs.

For the first two years of Daniel's life I actually managed to forget all about the Hellbrain.

But then we began to notice the delays in our son's development. By the time we celebrated Daniel's third birthday we had yet to hear him speak. He'd babbled when he was an infant; cooing at the various stuffed toys we'd paraded in front of him. But a chilling silence eventually replaced his budding voice. The specialists suspected autism, but told us that Daniel was too young to be diagnosed conclusively.

I first noticed the definite signs of my son being afflicted with Hellbrain on Labour Day weekend. Daniel was due to start preschool the following Monday, so the picnic supper Claire had prepared for us was a bittersweet affair; our baby was growing up. Halfway through the meal (cheeseburgers and seedless watermelon; two of Daniel's favourite foods), Daniel suddenly doubled over. His tiny hands were pressed against his eyes. Wads of chewed meat tumbled out of his gaping mouth. Was he trying to scream? Daniel rocked frantically back and forth, toppling over foam cups of orange soda. I flung myself around the picnic table and embraced my little boy. Claire reached over to take Daniel from me.

"... god ..." she whimpered.

Before I even knew what I was doing I'd driven my fist into Claire's chin. It was the first time I'd ever hit her, and the ease with which I did it made me numb. But Claire didn't complain. She didn't even react. Maybe she somehow understood. She just stood in the yard, watching me coddle my son, listening to me as I spat venom at whatever forces had hexed Daniel with my affliction.

Claire and I kept Daniel out of preschool that year. It was not a decision we discussed, but was simply something that we knew had to be done. Claire stayed home with him during the day while I worked as a file clerk in an accounting firm downtown.

Summer mellowed into autumn and things seemed to be improving for us. Whenever I had an evening off the three of us would go for walks or take Daniel to the playground around the corner. On colder nights we would stay in and watch TV: mainly sitcom reruns, sometimes game shows; any of the programs that Daniel seemed to enjoy ... and by enjoy I mean shows that he would sit still for while staring in the general direction of the screen.

A few months ago, while I was rummaging through the basement in search of Christmas decorations, a sour stench crowded my nostrils. It seemed to be leaking out from an obstructed corner of the storage area. I cleared away some cartons and the bicycles that Claire and I never used. A rubbery mound of blackish-red waste was piled in the corner. I knelt down to further examine the reeking pile. An unblinking eye glared up at me, its retina encrusted with grit and dust. The head it stared from appeared to have been a rabbit's. Random tufts of fur decorated the grisly remains. The rabbit pieces were strewn over a pile of decomposing rats. I also spotted a cat's tail but could find no body.

My son's name ran over and over in my mind as I hastily cleaned up the mess. I tossed the bagged remains in a nearby dumpster. I never spoke of it to Claire. Stupidly, blindly, I thought the whole issue would somehow resolve itself. If I kept the secret confined to some shadowed corner of my heart and never brought it out into the open, then perhaps the Hellbrain would be satisfied.

Three weeks ago Daniel attacked his mother.

One of the office's receptionists marched quickly into my cubicle and told me there was a hysterical woman holding for me on line two. I scarcely recognized Claire's voice. The only words she could manage were "Come home."

She was pacing the kitchen when I entered the house. Without, the sun had begun to wane, causing the unlit rooms to appear distorted, almost sickly. I moved to Claire and spotted the darkly-stained tea towel she had wound around her left forearm.

"I found him in the basement, where he'd been playing," she began. "He was convulsing, choking. I went to him ... and ..."

Her words fell away just as the tea-towel did when she tugged on it. A crater had been torn into the thick of Claire's arm. The jagged wound was rimmed with a crust of dried blood. Fresh plasma trickled out from several chewed veins.

"I had to kick him," Claire said as the sobs erupted from inside her. "His jaws were just clamped onto my arm. I had to kick him ..." with her good hand Claire pointed briefly at my groin, "there. And then I ran upstairs. I left him down there, John. I just left him there. He might be dead. Oh my god, I killed our baby ..."

I calmed her with a terse embrace, yanked a clean dishrag from off the oven handle and tied it around the wound.

"I'm going to get Daniel and then we're going to the emergency room," I said. Claire sank down onto the linoleum floor as if all her strength had just been drained away.

The basement door seemed immovable. I finally pulled it open; not really wanting to see what was waiting on the other side. Cool, must-tinged air spilled out to greet me. Only the first few wooden steps were visible in the darkness. For a second I was convinced that if I were to descend I would tumble headlong into an abyss. I slid my hand along the rough surface of the basement wall until I found the light switch. The naked bulb shone down on Daniel's tiny body, curled up like a seashell in the middle of the cement floor. For a moment I was certain that my son was dead. Strangely, I don't believe that any parent is ever utterly surprised when tragedy strikes their child. A parent's love is primal, ferocious. It can strip away logic and civility in a heartbeat. I've seen parents turn almost feral at the very *idea* of someone harming their offspring.

But parents also cannot help but think of horrendous things happening. I can't think of a day since Daniel entered the world where I didn't imagine finding him beaten to death, or seeing him getting hit by a drunk driver, or falling from a great height. You can't avoid entertaining these thoughts; they are what keeps you aware of the kind of world you're child is living in ... and they are part of what makes your child sacred. So when I saw Daniel crumpled upon the basement floor my initial thought was *'It's finally happened.'*

But then I saw his back rise slightly as he drew in a breath. I raced down the remaining stairs and knelt down beside him. He was sound asleep. His plump fingers and bow lips were both stained with Claire's blood. I scooped him up and rushed him and Claire out to the car.

The emergency room was crowded as usual and we wound up having to wait nearly five hours before someone (a first-year resident) tended to Claire's wound. Before Claire was released she had to speak to a therapist; an anorexic woman whose stringy blonde hair resembled sodden hay as it swept the sides of her skull-like face. She specialized in children with behavioural and psychological problems. In a tone that was so calming it was condescending, she relayed how crucial intensive therapy and behaviour modification were for boys like Daniel. I think Claire was still in shock, for she seemed to be unable to do anything but stare at the emptiness around her, her chapped lips wriggling as she uttered countless silent pleas. I humoured the child therapist by offering "mm-hmms" and nods and sickly-sweet thank-yous. Daniel sat in a chair, Zen-like in his centeredness.

I was overjoyed when Claire was finally released.

"There was something I forgot to tell you," Claire said apropos of nothing. We were stopped at a red light. The first few drops of rain splattered against the windshield. When I turned to face Claire the spots of rain mingled with the lights from the dashboard to lend her the appearance of a bluish cadaver infested with squirming insects. "When Daniel attacked me," she continued, "there was this weird light all around his head. It was cold. The light *felt* cold, do you understand? It terrified me, John." She paused, her voice quavering. She stole a glance of Daniel, who was staring out the window, oblivious and contented. "What are we going to do?" These were the last words Claire managed to utter before she broke out into sobs.

I should've listened to Claire, should've heeded her fears. But I've never been rational when it comes to Daniel. Against my wishes, Claire had shared all the details of our twisted saga with her mother and father. I had never gotten along with my in-laws at the best of times, but when Gordon dropped by the house one Sunday afternoon for a one-father-to-another rap session during which he urged me to institutionalize Daniel I began to foster genuine hatred for the man. What did he know about raising Daniel, beyond the condensed information Claire had given him?

When I adamantly refused to institutionalize my child, he told me that I was putting his child at risk and that he would never stand for that. The threat was glaringly apparent to me. I asked him to leave and he did.

The weeks went on, and I knew my illusion of normalcy and safety was beginning to dissolve, yet I couldn't bring myself to face the truth.

The cruel reality of the situation didn't even sink in when I came home yesterday to find Claire's mangled corpse in the upstairs hall.

Something was wrong that day. I'd known that from the very instant I opened my eyes. The sensation of impending disaster was palpable. I could feel it in my queasy stomach, hear it deep inside the tissues of my aching head, taste it; sharp and acrid on my tongue.

I'd tried phoning Claire from the office several times. I was worried, afraid even. I considered asking my supervisor if I could duck out early, but then a flood of work landed on my desk and my mind was pulled into the dizzying array of pointless tasks that one uses to fill their day. I somehow managed to convince myself that my anxieties about the day were due only to job stress, lack of sleep, and so forth. I didn't end up getting out of work until half an hour past closing time. I stepped into the house. It was cold and unnaturally still.

As I began exploring each of the rooms I felt as though I was touring some kind of carnival haunted house. I half-expected a masked figure to jump out from one of the darkened rooms, brandishing a plastic weapon. But I found my wife's mutilated corpse instead. The wet bits gleamed darkly in the moonlight. The pieces did not even look human, let alone like my wife. But I knew it was her.

I found Daniel once again sleeping soundly again on the basement floor, the monster returned to his dungeon for slumber. His chin looked as though he'd been mucking in Claire's make-up kit. But the smears were obviously not lipstick. His gore-gloved hands were folded to act as a pillow for his head.

I don't remember how the ball peen hammer wound up in my fist, but I do recall standing above my son with the tool poised, ready to be driven into his skull.

But I couldn't. It was quite clear that any killer instinct I'd once possessed had been bled out of me; passed on to the boy at my feet.

In the end I carried Daniel up to his narrow bed. He slept through the night and most of the morning, while I toiled in the basement like some mad character in a Poe story.

My child and I then fled the city.

*   *   *

"You're getting a bit of a paunch there, champ," I said, reaching across the booth to pat my son's solid belly. "We're going to have to sign you up at a gym, son. What do you think; do you want to be a bodybuilder?"

He looked up at me, albeit briefly and a sad thought occurs to me: Daniel would never know adulthood. Of course the romanticized vision of an eternal childhood is pandered by hack children's writers and by Hollywood, but the reality of it is heart-rending. In all likelihood, Daniel's condition would prevent him from ever knowing the touch of a lover. He'd never drive a car, or get drunk, or have children. He would always just be little Daniel, suffering and not knowing that he is suffering, because the Hellbrain was and always will be the only world he knows.

I wonder if maybe that's how it was for some of the other great 'monsters' of history; people who butchered dozens of other people. The ones were always well-liked by neighbours and co-workers. Was a monster's arrest not invariably followed by a flood of shocked acquaintances singing the hymn of I-never-thought-he-was-capable-of-this-such-a-nice-guy? Murder might be an all-too-human impulse, but perhaps the extreme cases, the ones for whom slaughter becomes an art-form, are really just possessed of Hellbrain; an impulse that creeps in from somewhere decidedly *not* human. It's a force so powerful that most of us can do nothing to stop it. We become little more than puppets for it, pawns.

I thought of these things and a lump formed in my throat. I pushed away my bottle of beer and fought back the tears that were brimming at the corners of my eyes.

A faint muttering from Daniel roused me from my sorrowful reverie.

"What's that, buddy?" I said sniffing back the trickle of snot that was threatening to run out.

"... *potty* ... "he said, half-looking at me this time.

"OK," I said, sliding out from the booth. "Let's go find the men's room." I reached to him and Daniel placed his chubby hand in mine.

I watched the other patrons watching me as I led a boy who walked on his tiptoes in order to study the red flicker of his novelty sneakers. I knew that to them this was a fleeting glimpse that would mark them; a chance voyeur into someone else's tragedy. For a moment I wanted each and every one of those gawking patrons to die. This wasn't some spectacle presented to them in order to make them count their blessings. This was my life. *Our* life; mine and Daniel's.

Discovering that the men's room was empty brought me some relief. I helped Daniel unbutton his jeans and then I waited outside the stall. I happened to spot my reflection in the soap-spattered window above the basin. I almost gasped when I saw the grey, haggard reflection staring back at me. Christ, did I look worn, sad; downright *old*. My skin felt leathery when I ran my fingertips down one side of my face. I would have given anything for a long bout of sleep; one that was gloriously free of nightmares.

A loud thud came from inside the stall. My body jerked from the shock of it. Another pounding sound immediately followed. A third.

"Daniel?" Barbs of panic pricked my insides. "Everything all right, pal?"

The stall door flung back and my son attacked me with a feral swiftness. I didn't even have a chance to brace myself, nor to shield my eyes or my groin.

Daniel was all teeth and talon-like hands. He was producing a howl that was both guttural and shrill. I fell back against the counter. He sank his teeth into the soft meat just beneath my chin. I screamed when he broke the skin. His spade-claw hand thrust toward my eyes again and again. I lost my footing and crashed to the scuffed tile floor. I looked up into my son's eyes, which had rolled back into his skull. Two white globules, like knobs of wet bone, stared back at me. His claws swung wildly. He was virtually blinded by a dark, primal urge.

It could've been a trick of the light, or a symptom of my pain and panic, but I swear I saw faint ripples of light emanating from Daniel's head; framing him like a Saint's halo in a stained-glass window.

I raised my legs to block the attack. Daniel bounced back off the soles of my uplifted boots. His head smacked against the cement wall with a sickening crack. He staggered for a moment, as though drunk, before finally crumpling into the stall.

I cried out. I pressed one hand against the wet wound on my throat and moved to Daniel. He lay crumpled against the toilet. He was dazed but still conscious. I pulled him from the piss-reeking stall and held him. I didn't care if he was still plagued by the killing urge; my baby was hurt.

The Hellbrain must have subsided. The blow to his head had probably snubbed it prematurely. I gently patted Daniel's head, feeling something dampening my palm. I peeled my palm from his sticky scalp. The sobs ripped free from deep inside me. I spun out a length of toilet paper, tore it from the roll and pressed against Daniel's wound.

Just then another man entered the washroom; a restaurant employee. I took his cheap polyester necktie as a symbol of managerial authority. He took one look at the two of us and his beady eyes widened behind his large spectacles.

"Everything OK? We heard screaming."

I did my best to keep both Daniel's and my wounds out of view.

"Yes. I ... I apologize. My son just had a seizure. He's all right now."

I lifted Daniel up and carried him out of the stall.

"Did you need us to call anyone? An ambulance? Maybe your son should just stay put for a while," the tie-man said as I moved past him.

All eyes were upon me as I moved to our booth to collect our coats and drop too many bills on the table to cover the meal. The speculative mutterings had begun even before Daniel and I had exited the diner.

We drove. The sun was beginning to dim. The sky was the colour of dirty dishwater. Daniel fell asleep in the back seat. Within a few minutes his head had stopped bleeding, which brought me some relief. Hospitals would have meant certain arrest, but I would have gone to one if Daniel had needed to.

I began to wonder where we could crash for a few hours. I might be able to drive all night, but couldn't go on indefinitely. Motels and inns would be too risky. I wondered what the odds were of finding an abandoned farmhouse or barn along these back roads.

I switched the radio on to usurp the thought-prodding silence.

Knowing that Daniel was in the back somehow made me feel even more isolated than if I'd been driving alone. I caught about ten seconds of music before the station went to its hourly news report. Claire's murder was their lead story. Daniel and I were both mentioned by name. I was a prime suspect but was nowhere to be found. It then became so clear to me that the reason why I'd felt so secure inside the diner was because they were piping in Muzak;

the whole restaurant was blissfully cut-off from the rest of the world. And the story was too fresh to have hit the papers. But I knew I was already the star of many dinner table conversations around the province. My arrest would inevitably occur; it was only a question of when. But when I thought about how I would react when they came to separate me from Daniel ...

They were thoughts better left alone.

My eyes felt grainy from fatigue. I could feel my head swaying like a lead ball upon my neck. The needle on the gas gauge was teetering precariously above 'E'.

By the time I spotted a small truck stop and gas bar at the side of the read my car was beginning to shake, threatening to die out completely. I glided under the fluorescent glow of the gas station awning. I glanced back at Daniel, who was snoring, his fingers gently kneading his jacket, which I had laid over him for a blanket.

"Be right back, bud," I muttered, though I knew Daniel couldn't hear me.

I was hoping that I could have paid for the gas directly at the pump using my bank card, but the equipment was almost comically antiquated. The interior of the truck stop was bright and barren, like the hull of a spacecraft in some B-movie. A lone figure behind the stout counter leaned over, I presumed to get a better look at me. I could feel his eyes upon me as I put the nozzle back on the rack and entered the building.

I nodded at the clerk, whose weathered skin reminded me of caramelized onion. I hurriedly snatched up some items from the dusty metal racks that stood in uneven rows: potato chips, bottled water, Pepsi, cans of soup and of beef ravioli, various sandwiches that were packaged in blue saran wrap. I withdrew three-hundred dollars from the bank machine, and then gasped at my own stupidity. My bank card would obviously be tracked. I'd just given my pursuers a beacon with which they would find me. I paid for the items and left, certain that the taciturn clerk was studying every detail of my appearance for future reference.

I moved briskly, trying to stifle my panic that was fighting hard to be freed.

When I reached the car the cage that held back my panic blew to pieces.

Daniel was gone.

The passenger door was a broken jaw that dangled open, exposing the sickening darkness of the vacant cab. About ten paces from where I stood, Daniel's jacket lay crumpled on the ground; a tiny colourful island amidst the drab grey ocean of gravel. I called Daniel's name, meekly at first, but increasingly louder. I ran to the side of the truck stop, hoping to see him wandering aimlessly. He wasn't there. I paused to listen for the telltale crunch of his feet upon the gravel, but only the sound was the soft hush of a chill wind that shook the limbs of the poplars that spiked the hills on either side of the road. I glanced at the dense woods that seemed to stretch unto forever. If

Daniel had wandered off, then I had to find him *now*, or, in all likelihood, not at all.

I crossed the threshold of the woodland. The lights from the truck stop were now as distant as the moon. I manoeuvred my way through the trees as deftly as I could, but the darkness made the wood labyrinth almost impassable. The trees grew in a semi-circle around the back of the truck stop. I followed the curve, theorizing that although Daniel might have entered the woods anywhere along this curve, he could have only gotten so deep. Assuming of course that he hadn't wandered into the road ...

"DANIEL?" I screamed, again and again. Hope was bleeding out of me with every clumsy footfall I made. Why the hell hadn't I checked the road first?

Two orbs of light flashed just off to the right of me. They flickered like two fireflies, but they were the wrong colour. Little red lights. Shrieking red lights.

I raced in their direction. But the lights just seemed to vanish into the night. I felt hopeless.

An amoeba of soft blue emerged from the trees and began to move toward me. I could just make out the balloon-like silhouette of Daniel's head.

Daniel's first blow blasted a shock of pain through my skull. I fell to one knee. My son's hand came down upon me again and again. A chunk of stone or something equally blunt must've been gripped in his fist. Like some Biblical confrontation, my son pounded his crude weapon against my chest, my face, the back of my skull. It splintered the bones in my hand when I tried to shield my head. I toppled onto my back. Daniel seemed to be hovering above me. An unnatural dawn increasingly brightened the night-time woods. I kicked wildly at my child attacker, but by this time the light was almost blinding. It, and my wounds, weakened me, made me delightfully woozy.

Then I heard it; a scarce fluttering of a voice.

"... *daddy* ... " it said.

Daniel sounded equally dazed, and just a little bit frightened, but also calm. I knew that the Hellbrain was fading. The torture I had passed on to my baby was finally beginning to pass.

The cool clear glow grew more intense as Daniel raised the dripping stone above his head.

"... *daddy?* ... "

He seemed lost, unsure what to do.

"Don't be scared," I managed to whisper, a bubble of blood muffling my voice. "Don't be scared."

The stone tore into my belly, and then shattered my collar bone. By now the light was blinding. I sucked in as much breath as my rib-punctured lung would allow, then gasped:

"Again ... "

The stone came down. Everything went beige, then grey, and then a shadowy drape began to fall. My last sight was Daniel falling back into a vast pond of soft blue light.

*   *   *

The clerk from the truck stop eventually found me. He told police that he'd gone looking for me after I'd seemingly abandoned my car at his station.

When I did finally regain consciousness I found myself lying in a narrow hospital room that smelled of ammonia and illness. My right arm was handcuffed to the bedrail. When I tried to lift my head, a policeman stepped into view from the dim corner where he'd been sitting.

"They found your wife in the basement," he told me. His voice was hard, almost robotic. "Where's your son? The judge might go easy on you if you cooperate."

My head fell back onto the pillow. I wished that I'd bled-out in the woods.

"We *will* find Daniel's body," the officer said, his certainty was absolute. His words barely escaped from between his clenched teeth. "You're going to burn for this," he told me.

I nodded. They could have me now. Daniel was safe. Nothing else mattered. Let them scour the woods, lock me in a cage, or strap me onto a table and push a needle into my arm.

Like so many murderers, I had found salvation. But the salvation I'd found was not my own; it was Daniel's.

My son has finally ascended past the Hell I'd forged for him. No matter what fate lies in wait for me, I'm nourished by the knowledge that Daniel has at long last risen to a higher house.

—0—

Even now, as he stood by the edge of the canal and smelled the exotic fragrances of the passing revellers whose rites were wholly bewildering to a foreigner like himself, Nathaniel Price's thoughts drifted back to his great Aunt Lydia's house in rural Ontario. Not even the crisp, copper-tinged dampness of Venice in late autumn could rouse him from his reverie. His mind's eye was oblivious to the present environment. Back and back it went, as steadily as the tides of iron-coloured water that slapped against the crumbling stone steps by the harbour …

—1—

In the half-light of February dusk, young Nathaniel Price watched eagerly as his aunt Lydia retrieved the box from its perch at the top of a Victorian pot dresser that stood just inside her dining room. Precious few lights were on inside the house, as was Lydia's wont. She preferred her world half-lit, for reasons Nathaniel was never able to ascertain.

Bitter winds moaned and whistled just beyond the grey brick exterior of the house.

"I don't know how many more times we can do this, Nathaniel," Aunt Lydia said, blowing the dust off the box's lid. The dirt swelled in the air, floating like a polluted cloud. Its dissipation was gradual. The room then became even dimmer, or so Nathaniel thought.

From the box Aunt Lydia produced a small key. Nathaniel knew this not because he could see it (he could not) but because he had gone through this strange ritual with his Aunt several times over the course of the winter and now knew it by rote. She would produce the key and then walk Nathaniel up the stairs to the topmost floor of the unusual farmhouse. They would take twenty-seven paces toward a locked door that loomed at the end of the hall. Aunt Lydia would then insert the much-guarded key into the door's lock.

But before she would unlock the door, there would be a painful hesitation during which she would study Nathaniel's face. Nathaniel was never sure how to react, or precisely what it was that his aunt was straining to perceive in his countenance, so he would often just kept his eyes upon the door, waiting for the doorknob to twist, the door to open …

But open it never did.

Aunt Lydia would invariably remove the key and rush Nathaniel back downstairs where he would then be encouraged to "amuse himself and keep out of trouble" until his mother returned to fetch him.

On this day, Aunt Lydia clutched the key in one hand and reached for Nathaniel with the other. Nathaniel followed her up the stairs, down the hall, and to the door. The key was produced. He could then feel Aunt Lydia's eyes upon him, and he then felt the natural impulse to gaze back at her. Lifting his gaze from the door, Nathaniel turned to look upon his aunt's dour expression, and into her black eyes. For a long, silent time they studied one another.

Aunt Lydia unlocked the door.

Nathaniel fully expected the door to groan eerily when Aunt Lydia did, surprisingly, nudge it open. But it did not. The door opened silently, which frightened Nathaniel all the more.

Aunt Lydia invited him to enter by a slight nod of her head, but the utter darkness of the room intimidated Nathaniel. Everything seemed softened, muted, by the blackness.

"There is nothing in the dark, Nathaniel, dear," Aunt Lydia said, almost musically. She bent down and repeated the phrase, this time placing emphasis on the word *'nothing.'* "Go and see, child. Go and see."

His initial step across the threshold was a timid one, but he soon found himself standing within the shadows that seemed to congeal like grease upon the ceiling and the walls. Light bled in from the hallway. It was weak, but still ample enough to allow Nathaniel a view of the unsettled dust that swirled upon the stale air, like the waves of a desiccated lake.

The room itself hosted two main scents: one being that of old wood, the other one not quite so obvious. It smelled vaguely like the inside of Aunt Lydia's old penny jar—coppery and cloying. The room's contents were minimal; only a small cot that stood very low to the ground. Its sheets seemed to be of varying shades of grey, though this could have been due to the poor lighting.

When Nathaniel felt the cold, smooth fingers coiling around his wrist, a flush of fear passed through him. Aunt Lydia tugged gently at his arm, guiding his hand to the pillow at the head of the cot. Nathaniel felt the softness of the pillowcase and the gritty sheen of dirt that covered it. He also felt two spots of cold hardness against the damp flesh of his palm.

"Pick them up," Aunt Lydia instructed; her voice a near-whisper. "Take them." Nathaniel snatched up the two objects, which felt like coins. He held them firmly in his fist. "Look at them."

He did. They *were* coins, ones that glinted like tiny suns in his palm.

For a long Nathaniel held the coins, studying them in a near-meditative trance; a trance that was harshly disrupted by the unexpected ringing of a doorbell.

"That must be your mother coming for you," Aunt Lydia said. She ushered the boy out of the room with what Nathaniel thought to be too much force, and then she relocked the door.

The bell rang a second time. Aunt Lydia leaned in toward Nathaniel and she spoke to him.

(Years later Nathaniel would come to realize just how closely his Aunt's gesture had been like the approach of a lover about to share some grand and guarded secret.)

"We won't be seeing one another for some time, Nathaniel," she whispered, "so you be sure and keep those coins safe, yes?"

Nathaniel did keep them safe.

During the drive home after what was to be his final visit to Aunt Lydia's, Nathaniel examined the coins keenly. They were actually much larger than ordinary pennies, and far shinier. In the passing yellow glow of the sodium lamps the coins appeared almost phosphorescent.

When he got home, Nathaniel deposited the coins into a small wooden box, which he had emptied of his baseball card collection. There they remained for seven years.

—2—

Two days after his sixteenth birthday, on the very night that he lost his virginity, Nathaniel received the telephone call informing him that Aunt Lydia was dead.

Elizabeth Kelly had been his girlfriend at the time. The two of them had been courting for four months. They were young but very certain of their feelings. Nathaniel's mother had gone out for the evening, so Nathaniel and Elizabeth used the opportunity to lose themselves in awkward passion.

Immediately after their urges were consummated, Nathaniel felt a sharp ache in his belly. Elizabeth had encouraged him to lie back on the bed, to breathe deeply. But Nathaniel's affliction was psychical rather than physical. It was the pain of impending tragedy.

Nathaniel had pulled himself up from the bed and, for the first time in seven years, retrieved the small wooden box from his dresser.

Later he would convince himself that what he had seen was simply the result of an over-stimulated imagination, but when he pulled the coins from their case, the copper face of Queen Elizabeth II was actually moving, like a crudely animated film. The surface of the coin bubbled and rippled as the tiny woman writhed about. Nathaniel could see her miniscule mouth gaping. He could almost hear her shrill scream.

The time immediately following this vision had become blurred in Nathaniel's memory. Apparently, the telephone rang. The caller was a neighbour of Aunt Lydia's who had gone to check on her, for she had not been seen in some time. The front door of the house was wide open. Once she realized that the house had not been burglarized, the neighbour went in to investigate. The neighbour found Lydia's corpse lying, arms folded, upon a cot in the uppermost room of the house.

Nathaniel had made good on his promise; the coins had been kept safe. He also came to understand their significance, and thus made arrangements with Lydia's mortician that she be buried with them upon her eyes.

—3—

We now move ahead to Nathaniel Price's thirty-third year. For although there were many pivotal events in the years between sixteen and thirty-three, suffice it to say that it was not until he was divorced, parentless, and financially destitute that Mystery finally returned to Nathaniel's life.

Shortly after Nathaniel's thirty-third Halloween, he came to the conclusion that he needed to sever all ties with the life he'd built for himself. He thought it best to do this consciously before his life collapsed in upon him. For the past year his life seemed to be teetering and swaying with an instability that caused Nathaniel many sleepless nights.

It had begun when Theresa had confronted him about his infidelity. Being a terrible liar, Nathaniel admitted that yes, he had been having an affair with a co-worker, and had been for some time.

The divorce was far more amicable than he'd imagined, but it nonetheless left him alone and low in funds. The co-worker that he'd been involved with ended their relationship shortly after Nathaniel moved into his own apartment. Nathaniel chalked this up to the fact that once their relationship had become legitimate the passion fizzled. The last he heard the woman was dating a man that worked in the company's accounting department; a man who, not surprisingly, was already engaged to another woman.

These events and others were Nathaniel's inspiration to use the balance on his credit cards to finance a ten-day trip to Venice. It was a rash decision, one that he would undoubtedly regret when it came time to begin actually paying for it. But it was important, perhaps even vital.

Even as he flew over the Atlantic toward the elder city, Nathaniel was unable to discern why he had chosen Venice as his destination. There were other cities he'd thought of visiting; everywhere from Kathmandu to Hollywood, but never Venice; particularly in the off-season. The travel agent he'd consulted had even advised Nathaniel to consider another vacation spot. "Venice is a bit weary-looking at the best of times," he'd said, "but in November, well ... I'm just concerned that it might be a bit too bleak."

But Nathaniel welcomed the bleakness. The fact that the agent then described Venice in autumn as "a veritable ghost town" convinced Nathaniel that he had chosen wisely. He'd pushed aside the lavishly-illustrated brochures for the Caribbean and arranged his flight for Venice.

It is only proper for a man to taste misery in his thirty-third year, Nathaniel decided. While waiting in the airport lounge Nathaniel realized that, in some small way, he was approaching his own customized Golgotha. Though he doubted that the effects of his journey would ever equal those of the messiah, he nonetheless found himself wondering whether Venice would bring him peace or a sword.

— 4 —

The taxi vessel bobbed its way across the Grand Canal. Nathaniel sat with his luggage at his feet, doing his best to shut out the merciless damp that seemed to loom all around him. He bunched the collar of his trench coat up beneath his chin in hopes that it would warm him.

Above, the sky was the colour of gravel. There did not seem to be any sun at all. Gulls and pigeons swarmed the sky and the eroded steps that sat flush with Venice's waterways.

Nathaniel studied the buildings on either side of the Canal, noting how each of them possessed the same weary, washed-out demeanour. The acidity in the air had eroded the coloured facades, staining them with unsightly bleached spots that resembled draining faces. Nathaniel began to realize that Venice was at once tragic and comedic.

The taxi sloshed its way around a sharp corner, nearly colliding with another boat that was speeding along in the opposite direction. Both drivers beeped their horns and shouted at one another in their mother tongue.

The taxi then passed a cathedral that was being guarded by two statues of what undoubtedly used to be saints. But the acidic Venice air had devoured the statues' features; reducing them to faceless spectres. Some of the ecclesiastical virtue seemed to have crumbled away as well, for the robed figures seemed to leer instead of gaze. Their fingerless hands might just as easily have been clawing as beckoning.

The driver slowed when the boat reached the Calle dei Fabri.

"Your hotel, she's on this street," he said. Nathaniel thanked him and paid the fare. Climbing out of the taxi and retrieving his luggage was a bit of a chore. The driver did not offer assistance. And as soon as Nathaniel had gotten all of his bags out, the taxi sped off.

Nathaniel walked to the entrance of the Al Gambero hotel and immediately realized why its rates were a fraction of its competitors. The Al Gambero was a narrow, gritty building. Its appearance caused Nathaniel to curse himself for not being a bit more extravagant on his accommodations. But the Al Gambero was on the bottom rung of the price ladder, and since this trip would tap him dry, Nathaniel had to be as frugal as possible.

He pulled the door open and stepped into a tiny foyer that served as the hotel's lobby. A rubber tree sat browning in a pot in one corner. Beside this was a desk chair with worn vinyl upholstery, which Nathaniel assumed was for any hotel guests. He walked to the tiny reception desk.

"You are American?" the concierge asked before Nathaniel even opened his mouth.

"No, Canadian."

"Ah, Canada."

"I have a reservation. My name is Price. P-r-i-c-e."

The concierge was a small man whose face resembled a boiled potato. It was oval-shaped, close-shaven, and embedded with eyes both black and beady. The man's eyebrows desperately needed trimming, for they frayed off of his brow like tiny feelers. His skin was very oily, and Nathaniel wondered if this oiliness was the reason why the concierge had managed to maintain a boyish complexion that conflicted with the noticeable stoop he walked with.

The concierge produced a ledger from beneath the desktop and began thumbing through it. He was muttering to himself and shaking his head as a sign of resignation. "Ah!" he said at last and turned the ledger to face Nathaniel. On the reservation page was the name "Pryze, N." Nathaniel nodded and showed the concierge the credit card number he had originally given to reserve the room. The concierge smiled and completed the registration.

The room itself reminded Nathaniel of a school dormitory he had been forced to stay in during a class field trip in fifth grade. But a dormitory room is designed to be strictly utilitarian, whereas this room had, at one time, been aesthetic as well as functional. But lack of maintenance had caused the décor to degenerate into a hideous parody of its earlier, purer form.

The room immediately conjured feelings of sorrow. It looked the way Nathaniel imagined a pauper's house would at Christmastime—a thin veneer of decadence stretched across a shrine of poverty.

The light streaming in through the window was filtered through a pair of white curtains. In order to lend the room an aura of cosiness, Nathaniel unpacked. He hung his extra trousers and his jacket in the closet and filled the small dresser with whatever clothing remained.

The lavatory was very cramped, with barely enough room to house the toilet and narrow shower stall. The tiles were tan; faded from too many bleach scrubbings.

A small basin was affixed to the wall just outside the lavatory. Nathaniel set his toiletries out on this.

By this time jetlag had begun to set in and Nathaniel settled into the bed with its too-soft mattress. He napped for close to three hours and awoke feeling even more drained than when he'd first arrived. The remainder of the night was spent alternately sleeping, staring out at the rain-tossed Venetian night, and yearning for things that defied definition.

The next morning Nathaniel managed to convince himself that he should make the most of the trip. He dismissed last night's malaise as culture shock, and began to explore the city at the first sign of daylight.

Venice seemed vacant. Many of the businesses were closed up for the season, or were operating at sufficiently reduced hours. At last he found a café that was open and went in for a breakfast of pastry and espresso. He had been hoping to purchase his pastries fresh out of the oven, but the baker had not begun the day's batch, so Nathaniel settled for purchasing day-old product at a discount. He had brought his guidebook to Venice along with him and he consulted it as he ate.

After flicking through the book's 'What to Do' section, Nathaniel realized that many of the listed events were seasonal. With considerably fewer options, he decided to make the Guggenheim Museum his first stop. Surely a few hours of solitude, surrounded by beauty, would lift his spirits.

—5—

The Guggenheim surpassed Nathaniel's expectations. After walking only a few paces past the building's marble columns he felt himself being transported to a strata that was far more serene than anything he'd known before, or certainly not since those enigmatic afternoons inside Aunt Lydia's gothic wonderland.

The colours were as rich as well-aged liquors. The atmosphere was bright and somehow purged of all modern confusions. Although not every exhibit appealed to Nathaniel's personal taste, he managed to draw at least some pleasure from each piece.

The tour's pinnacle occurred when he went to tour a series of paintings by Magritte, which were on loan to the Guggenheim from three other eminent art galleries.

All the Magritte paintings made Nathaniel feel as though he were studying a dream that had been ensnared in oils. But none affected him as much as 'Attempting the Impossible,' in which a young painter (a modern-day Pygmalion, no doubt) paints for himself the Ideal Woman.

The Woman in the painting—naked, serene and half-completed— somehow encapsulated every woman, or more specifically the perception of Woman held by the blunter gender.

Nathaniel stood studying 'Attempting the Impossible' for half an hour. He was so engrossed that it took him several minutes to realize that there was another person that apparently shared his silent reverence for the painting.

The woman on the bench could well have been the inspiration for 'Attempting the Impossible,' for her features were as serene. But unlike the figure in the painting, this woman was complete in every way. Aside from her natural physical beauty, the woman exuded an aura of spiritual wholeness. She sat stoically before the painting, not moving, not wanting. It was as if studying this single Magritte painting was the only worldly fulfillment she required.

Nathaniel found himself fantasizing about how the woman's flesh would feel, because from his vantage point it appeared flawless, marble-like; almost sleek. He imagined it as being perpetually cool to the touch.

The woman's hair was a very dark auburn and was cropped short; curling around her petite ears, draping her delicate brow. Her eyes were large and blue, her lips and nose were quite thin. She was dressed in a black skirt and a black blazer with glinting silver clasps.

Nathaniel studied her with even greater affection than he had afforded the Magritte painting. Other museum patrons milled in and out of the exhibit space, drifting past Nathaniel, who dared not move. He was neither certain nor concerned about how long he stood studying the woman who sat studying 'Attempting the Impossible,' but it must have been some time indeed, for the number of visitors had slowed to a trickle. Lunchtime, Nathaniel assumed, which made sense because he himself was rather famished.

"Would you like to have a drink with me?"

The woman's question was so unexpected that it took Nathaniel a moment to ensure that it was actually she who had spoken it. The two of them were quite alone in the Magritte area. The woman had turned her large eyes from the Magritte and toward him. Her unblinking gaze and staunch posture reminded Nathaniel of an Egyptian statue. And her eyes were quite like lapis lazuli at that.

"I'm sorry, were you speaking to me?"

"Yes."

Her voice was calming, free of any accent or dramatic inflections.

"I would love to have a drink with you."

She rose from the bench and linked her arm around Nathaniel's. As they strode through the galleries toward the Guggenheim's café, Nathaniel kept waiting to jolt awake in his dingy room at the Al Gambero. But, mercifully, the dream continued. It flowed on as the two of them sat at a small table in the café where they ordered drinks (espresso for him, Chianti for her.)

The conversation was more than a little strained. Nathaniel did most of the talking; about trivialities that he himself cared little about. He was only able to extract two pieces of information from the mysterious woman. The first was that her first name was Sophia, and the second was that she was lodging at the famous Gritti Palace on Santa Maria del Giglio. When Nathaniel asked her where she was from, Sophia stared into her empty wine glass like a tea-leaf reader preparing her soothsaying.

She then looked up and directly into Nathaniel's eyes.

"If you don't mind hailing a taxi for us, I would like you to take me back to my hotel."

At that point Nathaniel knew he must be dreaming, but he no longer cared.

The taxi tore across the Canal, but to Nathaniel it seemed to merely be lurching along. The boat halted in front of a building so ornate it actually made Nathaniel giggle. But any desire to drink in the wealth of aesthetics that the Gritti offered was dwarfed by Nathaniel's disorientation and by his desire to discover what his mysterious woman had in store for him.

Sophia strode through the hotel lobby, her stiletto heels clicking against the marble floor. Nathaniel scurried close behind her. He was certain that the guests and the hotel staff were staring at him as he joined her in the elevator. As the elevator ascended to the topmost floor, Nathaniel could not take his eyes from Sophia. She did not offer him even a single glance.

She unlocked the door to her suite and marched inside, leaving the key dangling from the brass knob. Nathaniel retrieved it, stepped inside and closed the door behind him. He turned to see Sophia peeling off her blazer and then her wine-coloured blouse. She unclasped her bra, removed her shoes, skirt, stockings and panties. Her skin was milk-pale and, to Nathaniel's eyes, flawless. Every curve was symmetrical.

Wordlessly, Sophia reached for Nathaniel, linking her fingers behind his neck. She pulled him closer.

—6—

Nathaniel was awakened by the ruckus of a crowd that seemed to be revelling somewhere in the streets below. He turned over to see Sophia lying next to him, staring at him in the half-light of the late afternoon.

"Did they wake you too?" he asked hoarsely.

"I wasn't sleeping."

Nathaniel pulled her form against his. He kissed the top of her head. Her scalp smelled of autumn foliage. "Sounds like quite a party," he said.

"They must be the early revellers. The Festa does not begin until Wednesday. Those people down there sound as though they're trying to get a head start."

"Festa?"

"Yes," Sophia said. From Nathaniel's vantage point her mouth looked like a red-rimmed abyss. "The *Festa della Salute*. It's celebrated in Venice every November."

"What is it, like Mardi Gras?"

"Not exactly. It commemorates the passing of the plague in Venice. Father Death made Venice his home in 1630."

"Well, that sounds like a lovely idea for a festival," Nathaniel said, hoping his sarcasm would be appreciated.

"Yes it is, isn't it?"

Sophia's sarcasm must have been far subtler than his, for Nathaniel couldn't tell if she was being serious or not. He pushed her chin up until her mouth met his. Sophia shifted under the covers and once more pressed herself down on Nathaniel.

—7—

It is to be expected that when Nathaniel Price woke up after the second bout of lovemaking he found himself alone inside the room.

For several minutes he was unsure of what to do. He felt nothing—not pain, not confusion, not fear. Somehow he knew that Sophia was not in the washroom, nor had she just run down to the lobby to retrieve something. She was gone.

'Is this what Aunt Lydia meant by the nothing in the dark?' he wondered as he sat amidst the gloom. The revellers of the *Festa della Salute* had evidently moved on, for Venice seemed eerily quiet, even for the off-season.

Nathaniel freed himself from the entanglement of bed sheets and searched for his clothes. He did not turn on a light. After he dressed himself, he found himself making the bed. He was unsure of the reason for this, except that he knew it would satisfy a compulsion. He slipped out of the room and found the key was still dangling from the brass knob. He freed it, slid it into his pocket.

He took the elevator down to the lobby and was about return the room key to the concierge, but at the last minute decided against it. If Sophia wanted the key, she would have to find him. He had to think back to recall if he had told the mysterious woman what hotel he was lodging in, and was relieved when he remembered that he had.

—8—

Despite his hopes, Nathaniel did not receive a visit from Sophia. Not during the following day, which Nathaniel spent playing solitaire in his dingy room. Nor the day after that, most of which he spent at the Guggenheim's Magritte exhibit. (His interpretation of 'Attempting the Impossible' had mutated; for he now viewed the woman as a horrible apparition, one that was rapidly vanishing from the artist who was only trying desperately to love her.)

Nathaniel tried to pretend that Sophia's rapid vanishing didn't hurt him, and in a manner of speaking it didn't. For, in a manner of speaking, Sophia was not absent from him at all: the city of Venice had become Sophia in one form or another. While skulking through its fog-padded streets at night, Nathaniel heard her sharp intakes of breath and the fluttery noises she'd made during the course of their lovemaking. When he surveyed the rows of old tenements, no longer did Nathaniel see eroding bricks and storm-bullied facades, he saw Sophia's flesh. Her alabaster skin stretched over the entire city. The Grand Canal itself flowed like the syrup of her cleft, the blood in her veins.

Nathaniel wondered when, if ever, this gale of memory would fade.

—9—

It was late and he was drunk. He was staggering along one of the many canals. He was counting the stones beneath his feet and inventorying the sundry woes of his life. Sorrow, it seemed to him now, was as certain and as changeless as the tide that sloshed up against Venice's rotting landscape.

A gondola suddenly whispered past him. Nathaniel took no notice of the gondolier, but felt quite dizzy when he spotted Sophia perched inside the boat. She was dressed in the same black coat with the silver clasps. A black kerchief was wound around her hair and face, lending her the image of a nun or a mourning widow. The gondola passed slowly. The oar seemed to slice the water noiselessly. Nathaniel wasn't sure what else to do, so he ran.

Later he would not be able to recall if he had called out Sophia's name or not, but he did remember his throat being quite hoarse after the chase, which ended only when the gondolier parked the boat before Redentore Church.

Nathaniel was stranded on the opposite side of the narrow canal. Sophia did not glance in his direction. She ascended the church steps, pulled its groaning door open, and slipped into its black confines.

Nathaniel tore his way across the nearest bridge. Redentore was so nondescript that he actually ran past it at first. He then quickly retraced his steps until he too was inside the musty, shadow-encrusted sanctuary.

A small candelabra flickered butter-yellow light against the front of the nave. The rest of the tiny church was dark and indistinct. Vague half-faces of various saints and martyrs studied Nathaniel as he crept down the aisle in search of the object of his obsession. He found her sitting in the front pew. She was the only entity in the church besides himself and the essence of the Christ.

Nathaniel stood at the end of the pew, frustrated with himself for not scripting the ideal statement for this encounter; the one he'd been mulling over ever since he woke up in Sophia's empty suite. But all the words dissolved like wind-sifted ash. Not knowing what else to do, Nathaniel sat down beside Sophia.

"Do you know what the problem with Venice is?" she asked after a bout of silence that was far longer than Nathaniel would have liked. "It revels in its own stratification from reality."

"Where did you go, Sophia?" He did not even bother trying to ponder her observation. All Nathaniel could think about was the bliss of her chilly body against his and the ache of that vacant suite that still smelled of her musk. "Why did you abandon me like that?"

"The water isolates the city, protects it in a way. It helps keep change at bay. The canals and the buildings; they all soften the edges of life, boundaries are blurred. Elements that are better left distinct are able to co-mingle here in Venice. The water also acts as a conduit, and that can be dangerous, don't you agree?"

"I never really thought about it," Nathaniel said.

Sophia spent another spell of time studying the bloodied face of the Christ statue, which looked positively macabre in the flickering half-light of the candles.

"Can we get out of here?" Nathaniel asked.

"You don't like churches, do you?"

"Not particularly. Come on." His fingers coiled around Sophia's thin arm. Nathaniel was surprised at this new-found sense of dominance. He practically pulled Sophia out from the pew and up the aisle towards the exit. He held the creaking door open for her. Its wood felt wet and foul beneath his hand. The gondolier was no longer out in front of the church, so they walked.

"Where are we going?" Sophia finally asked. Nathaniel had been nudging her down a number of side streets and alleys.

"I thought we could get a drink," was his reply.

"No, it is too early for that. Look, you can see the dawn already beginning to creep in."

"Well, we could go back to your hotel then."

"I'm not staying at the Gritti any longer, remember?"

"I know you left me there, but I've still got the key to your room, see?" The key glinted in the darkness.

"It won't do you any good," Sophia said, and before Nathaniel even knew what was happening Sophia snatched the key from his hand and tossed it into the canal. The sound of the key plopping into the water filled Nathaniel with rage.

"Fine," he said sharply. "We can go to my hotel then. Come on."

"No, I don't think so, Nathaniel."

"Why not?" His anger ebbed slightly, but a childish disappointment immediately replaced it.

Sophia did not answer him. She stood motionless, one hand clutching the black scarf that covered her head. In the darkness her face seemed to hover like a mask.

"Well, what would you like to do then?" he asked her.

Sophia did not respond.

"Can we go somewhere to talk?"

"That's not possible. As it is you should not have found me again, but as I said, these kinds of encounters are the nature of Venice."

She attempted to walk past Nathaniel, but he blocked her path.

"Wait! So that's it? You're leaving again?"

"Yes."

"No!" he shouted. By this time the fetters that had kept Nathaniel in check had snapped. The whole of his past become unbound. "I won't let you go. Every woman I've known has just up and left me right when I needed them. I'm not going to let it happen again, do you understand? Not ever again!"

Somehow Sophia was pinned against the alley wall. Nathaniel's hands tore at her clothing, mauled her flesh, yet he felt nothing. His senses were nullified as he tried to spread the woman's legs apart.

Sophia did not resist. She did not scream. She remained mute and limber. Nathaniel glanced at her face. There was something about her cold, stoic expression that filled his insides with ice water. The fetters of reason snapped his psyche back into place. Nathaniel realized what he was about to do ... and was crushed by the horror of it.

He collapsed onto the ground, sobbing.

"I love you," he whimpered, again and again. "I love you. Please, forgive me. I love you ..."

Nathaniel's hands were pressed against his face to prevent him from looking at Sophia. Blinded with humiliation, Nathaniel could hear the soft crunch of the woman's receding footsteps. Seconds later he heard the soft babbling of a gondola cascading over the waters of the canal at the end of the alley. He peeked between his fingers in time to see the dark vessel drifting into the haze of the flowering dawn. Cold water lapped gently against the steps. Somewhere nearby, birds were calling to one another.

—10—

It was nearly noon by the time Nathaniel came staggering back to the Al Gambero Hotel.

Although far from crowded, the streets were nonetheless peppered with whatever local merchants and guests there were in the city. They were all cheering and clapping. Lively music filled the air.

Nathaniel looked to the canal, at the parade of ghoulishly decorated boats that slowly paraded past the cheering crowd. He saw black flags snapping in the November wind, he saw the children with faces painted up to resemble decaying corpses. The air was choked with the perfume of funeral lilies. Streamers were tossed from the boats. They rippled through the air before landing on the water where they floated like Technicolor kelp.

People were shouting what Nathaniel assumed were well-wishes to him as he made his way to the hotel entrance.

The potato-faced concierge was standing in the doorway.

"Ah, long life to you, N. Priz-eh," he cried as Nathaniel entered. "Come and have a drink with me in honour of the *della Salute*."

"No, thank you."

"Come now. A bit of *vino, sì*?" He had already retrieved a bottle and two water glasses from behind the counter.

Too exhausted to argue, Nathaniel accepted the drink.

"Someone told me that this festival is to celebrate the plague," Nathaniel said, gulping down almost the entire glass of wine in one swig.

"*Sì*. Well, the end of the plague," the concierge said. "We dance and sing to celebrate death and life. Why were you not out watching the parade?"

"I don't feel much like celebrating."

"Well, there is only one thing that can make a man look the way you do now: a woman, yes? Let me tell you something about women, my friend." The concierge paused to pour more wine into Nathaniel's glass. Nathaniel was a bit surprised by the concierge's ability to speak English. "Learning to love a woman is a man's way of learning to embrace death."

Nathaniel laughed, but it was clear the concierge spoke in earnest.

"You do not believe me, my friend? Think of it, we love women because we know that we will not live forever; love them because we know that our time here is short. Ugliness and hatred; these are the great eternal things of the world. That is why we look to women; because even at their worst they are beautiful, and even when they lie they are somehow being truthful.

"Would you like to see the most magnificent thing in the world?"

The concierge took Nathaniel's silence as an affirmative response.

From the pocket of his wrinkled white dress shirt the concierge produced a small Polaroid. The paper was thick, its edges were rounded. It was the kind of photograph Nathaniel remembered from his childhood.

The subject of the photo was some kind of crude religious statue. The figure was crumbling and marred with vein-like cracks, like a half-melted wax effigy.

"The Black Madonna," the concierge said proudly. He took the photograph back and returned to the pocket above his heart. "I took this in a cathedral in France when I was a much younger man. I carry it with me always. You know why? Because the Black Madonna is holy; holy because she is flawed; flawed and fading away to darkness."

Even now, as he stood by the edge of the canal and smelled the exotic fragrances of the passing revellers whose rites were wholly bewildering to a foreigner like him, Nathaniel Price's thoughts drifted back to his great Aunt Lydia's house in rural Ontario. Not even the crisp, copper-tinged dampness of Venice in late autumn could rouse him from his reverie. His mind's eye was oblivious to the present environment. Back and back it went, as steadily as the tides of iron-coloured water that slapped against the ancient stones along the harbour.

He looked down at the water-logged streamers and the lingering confetti that created a festive scum upon the water.

Nathaniel reached into his pocket and fished out two random coins. He thought about what kind of doors they unlocked when, at the very end of things, they are placed upon one's eyes.

He thought of them as keys to something greater. Then he tossed the coins into the water.

{Dedicated to the memory of Robert Aickman}

His first memories are of movement; not an infant's crawl, but footsteps, graceful, almost fluid. As he wanders without apparent destination, the figure looks about him: surroundings dense with trees, with tight and gnarled thickets.

He looks about him and understands for the first time why the ash-tree is called such, for the limbs of these towering trees are brightened with the feverish hues of autumn foliage—scorching scarlet, searing yellow, lush and pulpy orange. The leaves, swayed by chill evening winds, flicker like torch-heads on the tips of haggard branches.

Surely their trunks are burned by these October pyres. Surely the reason their bark is the colour of a dead man's skin is because they've been burning for ages and ages. Charred and weak, now only the delicate ash remains of a world that once was—or a world that still may be in some autistic nightmare.

Looking past the trees, deeper, the figure notices for the first time that he is not alone. Other shapes, varying greatly in size and manner but not in constitution, flow and weave between the trees, above the trees, and through them. It's impossible to guess at how many nights and months and years are devoured by the journey, and those that stop to ponder this often parish. (Their bones click and clatter sadly in rainwater and in mud.)

Somehow a tiny cottage comes into view, nestled deep in the cavernous womb of a valley.

By this time the figure's thoughts have turned inward, so if there are others moving alongside him as he descends the winding path, he pays them no mind. Each step brings the pitiful cottage into sharper definition.

The structure is scarcely more than a collection of crooked, sagging eaves and rotted beams.

The porch groans as the figure advances toward the splintery door. The knob appears to be fashioned from a highly polished glass. Its manifold sides reflect the overcast sky like an infinite cluster of mirrors. Unlatching it, the figure can do little more than stare, child-like, as the door seems to glide open; parting the veil between this world and the next.

For an instant there is chaos as an impossibly large wasp flitters and soars upon the musty air inside the cottage.

There is a part of the figure that wants only to focus on the insect; to panic or to flee from the certain agony of its sting. Sadly, in most instances this timidity is the dominant aspect of the figure's being. In most instances ... but not this one.

For the figure's eyes look past the veil of chaos and into the deep and lightless throat of order. An order too vast for everyday consumption. An order whose every form is fleeting, whose every face is a mask.

The face of this particular order is that of a woman.

She stands so delicately that the figure is afraid even to breathe, for the slightest touch might dissolve this gossamer wraith. A wraith who does not, who speaks not, but simply is.

If there are words or thoughts or actions appropriate to such an encounter, the figure is ignorant of them. In lieu of these, he tries earnestly to convey an expression of understanding, or communion. Perhaps even of worship. And for that brief time he knows peace.

The woman dissolves all-too-quickly, melting from being into the shadows of non-being. Now only he remains inside the dank, lifeless room.

Tasting dread with a virgin's soul plunges him to near-oblivion. But the encounter had taken root in his mind and its repercussions flowed like nectar. They give him strength, urge him to take flight.

*   *   *

Time is a serpent, one that often constricts to choke the infinite out of its slaves. But somehow a few are daring enough to pry themselves free and slip through. And for that instant they can exist, *live*, outside the cage of time.

When the figure turns his head, the Time-serpent has re-coiled itself, for the cottage has aged even further and now scarcely stands at all. It is but a skeleton of charred beams.

Trying to clear his way through the debris is an arduous task, for time has webbed the ruins with a fleshy web that sticks to the figure like a hearty placenta; encumbering him with the contours of a man.

The journey is long, taxing, and what finally emerges on the other side is but a fraction of what first entered. The pitiless cycle of life has claimed much of the being who now continues to walk …

The sights of these new surroundings are far removed from those of the figure's original home. Great shimmering slabs of stone and glass have snuffed the fires of the ash-trees. Meat clogs the features of She Who Had Come.

The figure walks, for he has little choice. But those that walk alongside him are not like him. They cannot know what he knows, or perhaps what he now only dreams to be knowledge.

In spite of this, there are glimpses of what had come before; tiny confirmations of his sanity. Occasionally, amidst the drones, he finds another with a dark gleam to their eyes not unlike his. And in those moments, a wordless knowledge passes between two lost souls.

There are autumn nights when the air is perfumed with the lingering scent of wood smoke, and the bustle of the distant cities sounds remarkably like the buzzing of insects. On such nights, the contours of the moon gleam as She once did—bright and baleful and undying.

In my early years it was my family's custom to make an arduous journey every Yuletide to a cliff-top house composed of crumbling quarry rock. The house was perched upon a needle-like cliff that jutted out over what seemed to be a constantly raging sea. The air was always fragrant with fishy aromas; the wind invariably cold and wet.

My Great Grandmother made this place her home. In the latter days of December my relatives would congregate within its damp stone rooms. There the adults would drink bitter-smelling wines and converse in whispers. I can still recall the way the mantle in the great dining hall would be heaped with frothing green boughs, crunchy brown pinecones, graven images of the snow-bearded Holly King.

I remember how ageless my relatives seemed. The number of relations would swell annually. The family elders were always spry, always attentive, always eager to pass on exaggerations of the soft and sacred truths they'd learned in their unnumbered years.

While the adults mingled in the dining hall, the children were free to scavenge for the strange gifts that Great Grandmother would stash in the most obscure corners of her labyrinthine house.

Old rucksacks, drooping husks of reeking old fibres, served as the gift-wrap that concealed Great Grandmother's treasures. The sacks obscured the presents so well that it made guessing at their contents futile. I and the other children were forced to loosen the twine binding and plunging our hands (which were trembling, but not necessarily with excitement) inside to unveil our treasures.

Not all of the gifts were pleasant.

Yes, we would often unveil a small piece of costume jewellery, or a tin of chocolates. But I can recall one of my less-fortunate cousins reaching into the rucksack only to be embraced by the bristly appendages of a tarantula Great Grandmother had had imported from India. I personally will never be free of the feeling of plunging my fingers into a sack only to meet with the cold, slick jelly of a mare's heart.

Even if the gifts were not so macabre, the act of moving from chamber to chamber (sometimes with my sisters and distant cousins, sometimes utterly alone), would cause my breath to quicken. I would peer into musty-smelling curios, or beneath Great Grandmother's curtained bed whose four towering bedposts bore the faces of fanged old women and goat-faced children. Some of the rooms would glow with weepy torches, others hosted nothing but blackness. There was also the constant sound of the surf breaking against the jagged rocks a thousand miles below the house.

At the time I laboured under the impression that we were free to search any part of the mansion. So on that fateful Yule when I came upon a large key-ring in the pantry, I thought nothing of using the keys to further my explorations.

There was no question as to the door I would attempt to unlock first: The one that had always stood tauntingly shut in its jamb at the very summit of the mansion.

I moved to the narrow stairway at the rear of the house and began scaling the steps that spiralled toward the uppermost room; a chamber whose door forever remained secured with a chunky padlock. I had ventured up to that room alone, and although there were no torches burning in that particular stairway, there was a small arched window. The bluish glow of the moon afforded me a view of the lock, which I then attempted to open using each and every key on that enormous ring.

At last I found the proper one. I slid the spine-like key into the opening and felt the mechanism clunk. Pulling the lock free, I then dragged the door back from its frame. Unlike the other doors in the house, this one was composed of iron (heavily corroded) instead of wood, and as it scraped along the stone floor it screeched as if in agony.

The room it opened unto was a shrine of discarded items: armchairs and standing mirrors, clusters of broken toys and bundles of old paper, dummies dressed in moth-eaten gowns, and a very large steamer trunk that sat below an oval window.

Perhaps the trunk's proximity to the incoming moonlight is what first drew my attention. Its appearance was appropriately Gothic, but then so were all the other items in that musty storage room.

I became simultaneously drawn to and repelled by the steamer trunk once I heard the loud, deep and measured knocking booming forth from beneath its secured lid.

I was tempted to flee, to relock the weighty door, to return to the warmth of the torch-lit dining room. The cacophony of too many simultaneous conversations below was still vaguely audible inside the upper room. But the dominant noise was the repetitive thud that transformed that oblong box into a wooden heart.

I was frightened. I was burning with curiosity. Cautiously, I moved nearer to the box.

Other sounds, soft and subtle, then reached me; the scraping of fingernails dragging against wood; deep, mournful moans that reminded me of a distant foghorn.

I quickly added the jangling of keys to the thuds and the scratches and the groans.

I tried every key on the oversized ring, and when at last I felt the trunk's lock pop open in my hand, time halted. The noises from the box ceased, and suddenly all the timeless mysteries of Great Grandmother's house and of the night itself became concentrated on that Pandora's Box whose lid I then slowly pried open.

I did not recognize the gaunt figure that lay bound and muzzled inside the trunk. In the lunar gleam the man appeared to be a hundred-years-old if he was a day. The heavy wire—which was wound and rewound over the bluish skin of his body—glinted like spun silver. The man's eyes were wide, so wide they seemed lidless. They stared up at me, sparkling with wordless pleas for freedom.

I happened to glance down at the man's fingers, which were livid and capped with the ragged leavings of fingernails. I then spotted the slivers of his nails jutting out from the gouges in the box's sides, torn out by his own frantic clawing.

The man's vocalizations returned, but this time they were nearer to words than groans. However, the cast-iron mask that was clamped across the man's jaw made annunciation impossible. The bulging eyes glittered with tears. I watched one trickle down to the bristly mass of facial hair that sprouted out like crabgrass from beneath the iron muzzle.

"Did my Great Grandmother ... the old woman ... did she do this to you?" I asked. The old man answered with a slight nod of his head. Then the man began to sob; weak sobs that were stifled by iron. My heart ached with sympathy; and that's what made the removal of his muzzle so easy. I reached in and fumbled with the rusted clasps. I was shocked at how easily they gave.

I set the iron contraption down gently on the stone floor. The old man's jaws remained taut, and it was only after I massaged the sides of his head with my tiny fingers that the prisoner's mouth began to gradually droop open. He gasped with delight. His grey tongue pushed out over his flaking lips like a curious snail poking out from the safety of its shell.

"Thank you," were the man's first whispered words.

His next word was "Cutters."

He nodded slightly toward one of the many cabinets Great Grandmother had piled inside the room. I fished through the drawers until I found a pair of hefty cutters. These I used to clip the wires that had dug into the old man's flesh, and thus tethered him to the bottom of the trunk. The wire was thick and tough. My hands were throbbing by the time I managed to snip the last strand.

Freed, the man did not need my help in pulling himself up from his narrow prison. He stood ... no ... *loomed* over me, his body swelling to grotesque dimensions. It instantly eclipsed the moonlight. The room became a vault of sheer black.

A heartbeat later, I heard the shape scuttling out the open door.

The screams from the dining room sounded distant, yet also horrifically intimate. I fell to my knees, too shocked to move. I rocked back and forth, shivering, trying to focus on the sound of my own panicked breathing instead of the concert of death rattles that issued from my relatives at the bottom of the house.

I don't know much time elapsed before I finally managed to summon the courage to exit the tower room and descend the cragged stone stairs. I remember that all the torches had been extinguished.

When I entered the dining room I found my relatives slumped upon the floor, each one of them in a varying stage of decomposition. Some were ripe, barely cold; others were little more than a network of crooked bones lashed together by a few strips of rotted flesh.

Grand Grandmother herself was nothing but a pile of ashes gathered in the folds of her crumpled Yule gown. The ashes swirled lazily inside the draughty hall. The once-lush holly boughs hung limp and brittle from the mantle.

I wandered the halls of the house; muttering, sobbing; I think perhaps even laughing. Every so often I would inadvertently kick the corpse of a rat, or would round a corner and be startled by the appearance of another rotting relative.

Alone.

I began to wonder why I had been spared. Was it because I was responsible for unfettering something that was best left caged?

I staggered out of the house that now truly did stand at the edge of the world. I moved through the bitter night, to the edge of the cliff. I gazed down at the obsidian waters.

The slithering shape was like a dollop of curdled milk running down the rocky cliff toward the water. The thing's body was like that of a freshly-skinned animal, for its anatomy was plainly visible; a meticulous collage of dark slabs of muscle and organs woven together with a tedious network of dark veins; all bound with a sickeningly thin covering of semi-transparent flesh.

Suddenly the creature halted and turned its misshapen head upwards. I was grateful that both distance and shadows prevented me from seeing its face.

The thing then lunged off the side of the cliff; noiselessly parting the cold, black water. Damp winds soon carried the chloral stench of dead fish across the land.

Above me black clouds began to scab the moon and stars, snuffing them out one by one; plummeting my world into lightless tomb.

Standing on the cliff, staring out at the rippling void, ages seem to pass by, pouring over me like cascading waterfalls. I began to envision this cliff and that house as being wrought from numberless bones; bones that were heaved into this cosmic ossuary; marking the end of one age and the long, lightless span before the emergence of another.

Nourished by the realization that I am dwelling in the heart of a new silent aeon, I gaze down once more at the carpet of rippling onyx. But the fresh shadows do not allow my smile to be reflected, just as my voice echoes unheard inside this fortress of decay.

What Blooms in Shadow Withers in Light

I. CONCERNING THE KEEPER

The property had long been prone to lightning strikes, cattle mutilations, even a shower of falling stones. Yet no one but its owner; a stout spinster known to the locals as Miss Prudence, was aware of such phenomena. She alone had experienced these diabolical miracles; she alone was cognizant of their purpose.

At dawn Miss Prudence steps out her front door to survey the expanse of her withered farmland. The air is simultaneously mild and chilling, as it so often is in October. She shuffles out to the edge of her drooping front porch, wrapping her fingers (which arthritis has rendered into plump, misshapen stubs) over the railing.

Nothing appears to have been altered during the night. The soil bears neither cloven-hoof print nor trails of shimmering slime. The air does not reek of brimstone. The thin twining of wolfsbane and garlic flowers remains intact over her front door. And, most importantly, the great grey barn that is slumped in the centre of her farmyard appears to be intact, which means that today's work may not be as dangerous as Miss Prudence had initially feared.

She descends the steps carefully, and the wood groans under her weight.

Across the dew-soaked grass, then over to the barn.

The property has been in Miss Prudence's family for generations. She, like her ancestors, had been raised to be wholly self-sufficient. With the farm being a nexus of unnatural elements, the fields have long been scourged of whatever nutrients they once possessed. The meagre crops Miss Prudence did manage to harvest were scarcely enough sustenance for herself. She sells any leftover produce to those passers-by who pity her enough to purchase a basket of withered apples in the autumn or parched peaches during summer. It is an archaic way of life, but it is the only life Miss Prudence knows. Had fate been kinder, Miss Prudence would have adult children ready to take over the sacred family duty of Keeper; a duty that the family had begun to execute with fierce diligence during the Dark Ages, but less maniacally since the Industrial Revolution had sharpened men's minds as well as their material appetites. (Keen thought and covetousness had managed to level most of the superstition that had once thrived in the world.) But Miss Prudence has been so immersed in her Work that time managed to slip by her unnoticed. She is now just two months shy of her seventieth birthday, and has no hope of continuing the Keep, no prospects for personal happiness, no indication as to the destiny of the race she has spent her life protecting.

She reaches the barn door and pauses to listen to the slithering, to the growling, and to the howling that bounces from rotted wall to rotted wall.

Taking the small sack down from its hook on the barn door, Miss Prudence begins to sprinkle a fresh ring of salt around the building. She wonders how much longer these bitter little crystals can hold them; all the tentacled things, the many-legged things, the things with arachnid bodies … or worse; no bodies at all.

If only she had others to help her, she could have taken the time to learn new techniques, new binding spells, new banishments.

If only …

She begins the opening rubrics to guard herself against the onslaught that would occur at dusk.

II. FROM MEPHITIC ASH, A SAVIOUR

Aptly, the evening sky resembles an inferno; all livid orange and scarlet and ash-grey. Its fuming half-light endows the numerous decorated homes in the town of Greyleaf with a mock-animation. Bed-sheet phantoms snap and bob upon the chill breeze, each one struggling to free themselves from their tree branch traps. Plastic gargoyles seem to stir upon their porch step perches, hungrily leering toward some tender prey. Cardboard black cats arch their backs in defiance. Rubber replicas of movie monsters nod in agreement over some unspoken pact.

A tiny shape (only slightly more human than the decorative grotesques that line the street) plods along the sidewalk. A padding of desiccated leaves crunches beneath the soles of his work boots.

The wind carries omens of the coming winter. It penetrates the worn fibres of the figure's coveralls, but the figure is unfazed; for tonight is pregnant with potential for men like him; those possessed of shadowy appetites.

Both of the man's hands are full: one clutches the steel lunchbox he uses to cart his frugal meals to the plant each morning, the other lugs a cumbersome plastic grocery bag whose overstretched handles dig into the meat of his fingers.

The figure (a small, stout man with a pronounced chin and a balding cranium) was, in youth, called Otto. But age has earned him the more official-sounding title of Mr. Umbra.

Mr. Umbra shuffles up the steps of his front porch. His house is tiny, its contents sparse, its decor painfully utilitarian. The red brick exterior hosts no decorations whatsoever.

He balances the grocery bag on his left thigh while he searches through his pockets for his house keys. Unlocking the front door, he slips into the murky stillness of the empty abode. Shutting the door on the outer world, Mr.

Umbra steps gingerly down the hallway, feeling the plastic bag beginning to split, threatening to spill out its precious contents. He enters the kitchen just in time, plopping the shredded bag onto the counter with a thud before hurrying back to lock the front door and sliding the security chain into place.

Mr. Umbra tends to his duties in the kitchen.

Rummaging through the semi-clean dishes that sit in a rack beside the sink, he selects an appropriate knife and sets it down on the Formica countertop. The remnants of the plastic bag are peeled away to reveal a single package of Halloween candy and a rather poor specimen of a pumpkin. One side of the shell appears to be caving-in from decay. The black-green-orange rind is perforated with wormholes.

'Serves me right for not shopping until October 31st,' Mr. Umbra thinks to himself as he jabs a dull kitchen knife into the top of the pumpkin and begins to saw. He hollows the gourd of its pulpy innards, most of which stink of rot. Giving little thought to the design of the jack-o-lantern, Mr. Umbra opts for a simple design. He slices out two triangle eyes, a lopsided triangular nose, and a sneering zigzag mouth.

Cursing himself for not remembering to purchase a candle, Mr. Umbra resorts to using one of the tiny white candles from his blackout emergency kit, which he keeps in a cupboard above the stove.

He empties a cereal bowl of that morning's bran flakes and milk, rinses the dish under the tap, and then fills it with the meagre selection of candy.

With the trappings of his outer temple now prepared, Mr. Umbra readies himself for the second, and far more crucial, inspection; that of his secret inner temple.

He makes a quick jaunt to the upstairs bedroom to retrieve the spiral-bound notebook from his nightstand. This he carries down into the cellar. Weaving through the basement's labyrinth of cardboard boxes, bundles of old newspapers, and pieces of broken furniture, Mr. Umbra finally reaches the hatch-door in his cellar floor.

There is a string that never leaves his neck. It holds the keys for the hatch-door's padlock. Mr. Umbra loops the string around his finger, pulls the keys out over the collar of his coveralls and unlocks the hatch.

The room it opens unto is tiny but equipped with all the essentials—a narrow cot with a pillow, a standing lamp, an electric fan, a baseboard heater, firm manacles that are bolted into the stone wall and the floor.

Mr. Umbra opens the notebook and thumbs through the pages that bear his shaky handwriting; squiggles that sketchily chronicle his nightmares. His eyes alternate between the barely-legible notes and his subterranean inner temple. Ordinarily his work ethic is slipshod, his attention to detail almost non-existent; but as he gives the inner temple one final inspection, Mr. Umbra is warmed by the knowledge that he has executed this particular project with rare meticulousness and dedication.

The distant laughter of children becomes audible through one of the blacked-out basement windows. Mr. Umbra hurries (as much as a man like him *can* hurry) upstairs to the kitchen. There he lights the white emergency candle and inserts it into the jack-o-lantern. He carries it and the tiny bowl of candy out to the front porch.

With some difficulty, Mr. Umbra props the lopsided pumpkin against the porch railing and then eases himself into his battered porch rocker. There he sits, waiting, running his fingers through the psychedelically-coloured candies in his cereal bowl.

Twilight wanes and shadows lengthen. Mr. Umbra waits. Each pack of giggling trick-or-treaters sparks a hopeful excitement in him, but after examining their costumes, their gestures, their demeanour; Mr. Umbra is saddened to discover that the dream-child is not among them. To these undesirable urchins Mr. Umbra sulkily tosses little packets of chewing gum or mini chocolate bars before he shoos them off his porch.

He runs out of candy in less than an hour, but he remains on his porch until the white emergency candle burns down to a useless blob of wax inside the rotting pumpkin. The night grows winter-crisp, the stars glint like ice from behind woolly black clouds.

It is while Mr. Umbra is preparing to toss the pumpkin into the trashcan at the side of his house that the child arrives, crying out "Trick or treat!"

Mr. Umbra pauses, the pumpkin still in his hands. He looks upon the tiny grease-painted ghoul that sheepishly scales his front steps.

Mr. Umbra smiles.

"Trick-or-treat," the monster repeats, softer this time. A shudder of bliss runs through Mr. Umbra.

"I have something *very special* for you, Mr. Grave-robber, sir," begins Mr. Umbra. "Now, if you'd be kind enough to step inside my haunted mansion …"

III. TWILIGHT'S FRAGILE GUARDIAN

Miss Prudence is so grateful to see the first signs of the All Saints' dawn on the horizon that, for a moment, she almost convinces herself that the sun's ascension is illusory. She studies the ribbon of orange; a tiny ember glowing at the heart of the darkest night of the year. It begins to dilate, casting wide beams of illumination over the woods and the nearby farmyards.

From her hermetically-sealed barn come yowls of defeat.

Miss Prudence raises the rosary she's been clutching in her crooked fist. She presses it to her lips. This year's banishments had been the most difficult ones she could remember. More than once the barn looked as though it was about to tumble, more than once it seemed that its captives would be freed.

There but by the grace of God ...

Drained and teary, Miss Prudence staggers off to her warm bed, muttering ecclesiastical praises.

IV. COLD PROPHECIES

Mr. Umbra glances out the snow-bearded kitchen window, at the February blizzard that stirs and lashes the world outside his home. The wind moans. Ice pellets patter against the glass in rhythmic blasts. Mr. Umbra shivers, pulls the threadbare cardigan tighter around his plump belly. He turns his attention back to the saucepan of turkey soup that is heating on the stove. He gives the milky broth a stir and then pours it into the same chipped cereal bowl he'd used to dispense candy from last Halloween. Mr. Umbra picks the bowl up cautiously, tucks a box of cheese-flavoured crackers under his arm, and makes his way to the cellar.

Weaving between the basement's clutter while carrying an overfilled bowl requires savvy; something Mr. Umbra lacks completely. The hot broth sloshes over the bowl's rim, scalding his hands. He curses under his breath. When he reaches the hatch door, Mr. Umbra sets the bowl and the box of cheese-flavoured crackers down on a battered carton containing unused yuletide decorations. He slides his grub-like fingers beneath his shirt collar.

The child hears the fat man beyond the door, fumbling with the lock again. Quickly, defiantly, he tosses the notebook underneath his cot.

Perhaps this way the fat man will not ask him about his notes. Out of sight, out of mind. Perhaps he would be spared, just this once, of having to recount the horrors of his dreams.

After so many months the child had grown accustomed to living inside Mr. Umbra's inner temple, but he still did not believe the little man's theories about the Saviour, or that the little man had actually dreamed of his arrival; right down to his ghoul costume. Such things seemed foolish to the boy, even though in some ways it did explain why he was never found by his parents or by the authorities, and why Mr. Umbra had never even been a suspect in his disappearance.

And lately the boy *had* been experiencing dreams—dreams of a distant place; of black forms slithering toward freedom, toward dominion.

The lock gives and the fat man staggers into the cell. He is balancing a bowl against his bulging belly. The smell of the soup reminds the boy of his mother's kitchen in a house at the other end of town. He thinks of the copper pots that decorated her kitchen walls. He thinks of these things and his eyes sparkle with fresh tears.

The fat man sets the bowl down gently on the lopsided folding card table that stands at the foot of the cot. The spilled broth forms sickly yellow puddles on the tabletop.

"How are you feeling tonight?" asks the fat man. (His voice is disturbingly high-pitched for such a large man.)

"Cold," answers the boy.

There is a low whistling sound as the fat man breathes through his nostrils. Is he deep in thought?

"I will bring you some more blankets. I think I might have another space heater, too. I'll look for it before I go to bed tonight. Now," the fat man wagged his thick hand, "your notebook please."

The boy reaches for the tarnished spoon and his shackles chink in the darkness. He pierces the congealed film floating on the soup and spoons up some of the steaming broth underneath. The spoon is halfway to his mouth when the boy feels the fat man's enormous hand coiling around his wrist.

"Please," the fat man says in a tone that is at once both quiet and forceful, "the notebook."

Hunger pains twist the boy's insides. Reluctantly, he sets the spoon down and reaches under the cot. He gropes about the cold, un-swept stone floor until he feels the gritty cover against his fingers. The boy slides the book out and hands it over to the fat man, who immediately frees the boy's wrist.

The boy gulps the soup up greedily.

The fat man flicks through the ink-tattooed pages just as greedily.

Neither one finds satisfaction.

"These squiggles and curlicues," the fat man announces after a long, oppressive silence, "do they mean anything?"

"Yes," answers the boy.

"Really? What?"

"I dreamt of them, on a barnyard wall. They were written there in an old woman's blood."

The fat man actually moans with delight. "And?"

The child shrugs. "They were just symbols, but in the dream I could read them. In the dream they read: '*It will unfurl this All Hallows ...* '"

The boy can see the fat man's teeth as he grins; they are slick with saliva and are as grey as tombstones.

V. FATE MANIFESTS, DARKLY

It is unseasonably warm on this October 31st. Miss Prudence awakens in a sweat-drenched bed. Could the weather be an omen?

Miss Prudence thinks of last night's dream, and shudders.

"Really now," she says aloud, disgusted by her own susceptibility, "really, such dreams." Enough of this grim and bloody dream-stuff; there are preparations to make before tonight's Binding.

Her hands are shaky, her head light. It is going to be a long day indeed.

She makes her way down the hall to the bathroom where she washes her face. Then, downstairs for a cup of boiling water to aid in her bodily purification. She puts the kettle on the stove range and waits for the water to boil. 'Silver tea' was what mother had called it whenever she'd served it to Miss Prudence as a child. Sometimes mother also used to give her communion wafers to munch on. Other times she'd give her herbs. Those had been happier times.

Miss Prudence shuffles into the sitting room and retrieves one of the large diaries from the bookcase. She carries it back with her into the kitchen and, after pouring her silver tea into a mug, she begins to read over the details of her mother's battles with the powers of darkness.

Flicking through the brittle leaves, Miss Prudence wishes she had a photograph of her mother. Of course she knows full well that snapping a picture would have thieved her mother's soul, but Miss Prudence is nonetheless pained by the way her mother's face is beginning to fade from her memory. She suddenly wishes she had maintained notes of the noble conquests she herself had made in the name of the Prudence family. But then, who would read them?

"All things end," sighs the old woman, closing the diary. The distant howling rouses her from her reverie. She rises and begins to prepare for the annual Binding.

VI. INTO WHOSE HANDS?

The bus barely makes it across the final state line before its radiator hose blows, shooting fluid and steam out across the dirt road.

At that moment Mr. Umbra temporarily loses faith in the operation. It is the boy who centers him.

"We can walk to the farm from here," the child explains.

"You sure?"

"I'm sure."

It is late afternoon. The sky is heaped with heavy clouds. The cold-warm air smells of earth and wood-smoke.

"The old woman has them trapped in a barn nearby," the boy observes. "They're … anxious."

The two of them stand for a moment or two, gazing into a skyline that is the colour of decomposing flesh. As if on cue, they simultaneously resume walking.

"You know," says Mr. Umbra, "all the things I did I did as an act of service; service to you as well as them."

"I know," replies the boy.

"It wasn't something I necessarily *wanted* to do, but strangely enough, it was something I *chose* to do. It was a blind choice; deciding to intercept you and allowing your fate to flourish. But I think I made the right decision."

"Did you really dream of me, of all of this?" asks the child.

"Yes."

The boy smiles sweetly.

Although she'd been ailing for the entire day, Miss Prudence doesn't experience the actual attack until she spots the child and the man making their way up the road that winds, snake-like, between two sprawling pumpkin patches. She collapses as something powerful squeezes the tender jelly of her heart. Salt and holy water spill uselessly onto the soil.

The captives inside the barn squeal with bestial delight.

This cacophony is the sound that Miss Prudence takes with her to the next world.

Mr. Umbra follows the boy partway onto the property, but then halts. He is taken aback by the terrible sounds from the barn, but the boy is not; he moves with grim determination.

The wood of the barn door groans, it throbs like a splintery heart. Then it *bursts* like a boil; spraying wedges of ancient wood and alchemically-treated wax seals across the desolate fields of the Prudence property. By this time dusk has fallen and the land is washed in a purple-orange glow.

'Free!' the things seem to hiss. *'Free!'* The slithering things and the scaly things and the things that are but fog and whispers.

The boy sees them. He whimpers with joy, with awe.

Mr. Umbra sees them also, and bows his head.

The shapes swim upon the swelling darkness of All Hallows. They clamour up twisted trees, they hover on brimstone-tinged mist. They take flight with sprawling wings. They burrow swiftly under the scorched earth.

Not even in their blackest reveries could Mr. Umbra or the child have expected the Unbinding to be so glorious.

But it was only the beginning.

"Gone," the boy says breathlessly when he at last joins his companion, "they're all just ... gone."

Mr. Umbra is bent over, breathing heavily, his sweaty palms are pressed against his knees. "Yes," he gasps. "Migrating. Just for a little while. Most people aren't ready to greet them yet."

After a time the boy asks, "So that's it then?"

Mr. Umbra shakes his head.

"Not if my dreams are to be believed," he says. "They should have left some things for us in the barn," Mr. Umbra explains as he produces a small velvet pouch from the pocket of his trousers. "We need to go in and collect them."

"And then we burn it?" asks the boy.

"To the ground. But first we have to search, *really* search."

The child sprints to the barn and obediently begins inspecting every inch of its dark, reeking interior. Mr. Umbra searches also; first inside the woman's house for a flashlight (which he does not find, but does discover a small kerosene lamp which suits his purposes just as well), and then with the boy inside the great wooden fortress. By ambient lamp-glow the two of them rescue sprouts of wiry hair from a bedding of mouldy hay. They pluck torn nails and talons from the gouges in the barn door. They peel gelatinous scum from the summit of the loft.

Mr. Umbra intones quietly, "So it is done. So it shall be." He tugs at the drawstring on the velvet pouch, closing it.

The child accepts the lamp that is passed to him. He raises it above his head and then glances at Mr. Umbra, who nods his approval. The glass casing of the lamp shatters on the barn floor, sending thin fingers of flame across the hay and the warped planks.

Mr. Umbra and the child exit the blazing property without comment.

VII. HALLOWED HARVEST

The soil of the tiny lot is flecked with glinting frost as the child and Mr. Umbra prepare to dig on that cold November dawn. They shovel a pocket into the black soil, and into this pocket they deposit the nail fragments and the wiry hair and the sludge. They bury them, pat down the soil and mark the area with a chunk of polished hematite.

"And now," Mr. Umbra announces as the boy helps to pull him up from his squatting position on the soil, "we wait."

And wait they do—through the remainder of that smoky, leaf-rustled autumn; through the grave-cold stillness of the long, long winter; through the brief, marshy spring and the subsequent searing summer.

The boy stayed cloistered in Mr. Umbra's tiny house. In the daytime Mr. Umbra worked his simple job. Sometimes in the evenings he and the boy would share their dreams with one another. Sometimes they'd play Scrabble. Sometimes Mr. Umbra would read his books while the boy watched television.

The two of them waited until the world once more turned grey and dank with mystic shadows.

October. Then and only then did the two of them return to the meadow where they'd planted the remnants.

The tree has grown with unnatural swiftness. Its trunk is large and firm, its branches thick and lengthy. The bark of the tree is white; as the harvest moon or as fresh bones. It is porcelain-smooth to the touch and smells of rain and charnel house pyres.

The tree's apples grow in great ripe bunches on the boughs. In contrast to the pale tree, the fruit is onyx-black. The apples shimmer darkly, reflecting the constellations of the night sky.

"Is it like your dream?" the boy asks.

Mr. Umbra finds it difficult to speak at first. "Yes," he replies, "exactly."

Methodically, the two of them collect their harvest.

*　　*　　*

"Trick-or-treat!" cry the goblins, the witches, the little giggling Father Deaths.

The boy steals peeks at the procession, shielded by the living room drapes.

Soon the world would be safe for him to walk freely again. Soon, but not yet.

Mr. Umbra sits on the porch. A large basket rests upon his lap.

"Aw, an apple," huffs a small red devil when the treat is handed to him.

"Oh, not just any apple," replies Mr. Umbra. He rotates the black fruit slowly before the child's eyes. "This is a very special All Hallows apple. It's magic."

"There's no such thing," rebuts little Lucifer.

"What a thing for the Father of magic to say!" Mr. Umbra laughs then leans toward the child. "Confidentially, you are absolutely correct, Mr. Scratch. There isn't any magic. Unfortunately, I can't seem to convince any of these stupid children, so I need your help, OK?"

The child nods.

Mr. Umbra continues: "I want you to promise me that you will eat this delicious apple before you go to sleep tonight, so that when you wake up tomorrow morning you can *prove* to all your silly schoolmates that magic is a sham, that apples cannot give a child magnificent nightmares. Do we have a deal?"

The devil-child looks at him bewilderedly, but takes the apple just the same.

The other children do not seem to be as sceptical as Satan. They are all eager to sample the black fruit that can only be eaten (or so they are instructed) *"when you are alone, in the dark, and ready to slip into slumber."*

Later, as the first few snowflakes of the season begin fluttering down and the last few "Trick-or-treat" cries of the season begin to fade, Mr. Umbra blows out his Jack-o-lantern and steps inside. He is actually giddy; chortling to himself and humming an improvised tune.

That night only a dozen or so children actually follow the strange fat man's instructions, but it is enough to begin the Change.

These children—some of which are daring, others merely superstitious—crunch their black apples in the sanctuary of their bedrooms, relishing the candy-sweet pulp as it melts upon their tongues.

Cozy table lamps are then switched off. Novelty skeleton-finger candles are puffed out. Heads recline onto pillows. Fresh minds open unto Nightmares.

And the open-mindedness of these Nightmares allows something *else* to slip inside the dreamers.

The cycle begins slowly, but not unnoticeably. For how long can a parent dismiss the nightly screams of their child as he or she is ripped from sleep by unearthly images? How long can the rash of diabolic visions documented in tabloid journals and religious tracts be laughed at or discarded?

As all things slip, swiftly and inexorably, toward a new Dark Age; one whose laws are dictated by the vague and nameless forms that creep in from the distant margins of the night, two figures wait to hear the heralding howl; for only then can they enter the darkness and lose themselves. Only then can they enter the darkness and be found.

If you'd been ill for as long as I'd been, you also would've made the pilgrimage to "Professor" Keep's shabby little office on the outskirts of Thornton.

That damp night, as I explored the narrow roads which coiled through Thornton's beach strip, cold feelings of disillusionment twisted eel-like in the pit of my stomach. A number of weather-bullied cottages were the only visible structures in the area. Unkempt foliage frothed over the wire fencing that lined the roadways; blackish leaves gleaming with jewels of dew under the moon.

I paused amidst the swirling mists to muster up the energy needed to continue my search. Extracting the crumpled brochure from my jacket pocket, I compulsively rechecked the address, musing that Keep's office should be fairly close by. I hoped to find it in time for my nine o'clock appointment. The image of my warm bed flashed through my mind, and in my exhaustion I found myself thinking that I would never see my home again. I purged this idiocy with a shudder and resumed walking.

After too many twists and turns I finally spotted an ominously tall, yet comically narrow, house whose large front window was brightened by the stark whitish glow of an uncovered light bulb. A set of three wooden steps communicated the house with the dirt roadway where I stood, rethinking my decision to visit the self-proclaimed "Metaphysical Healer" whose secret therapies had earned him a cult of devotees among the sick and the hopeless ...

*   *   *

I first encountered the name and reputation of Benjamin Keep through Roberta Twiss. Twiss was the owner of Wise Alternatives; a humble boutique that purveyed all-natural herbs and medicines as well as many books on the subject for those who wished to look beyond the modern medical industry. Prior to my contracting abdominal cancer three years ago, I regarded homeopathy and the like to be as foolish (and as ineffective) as voodoo or good-luck charms. But once the wonders of science had eroded my body to a ghostly shell of skin and bones, and had almost erased my will to live, I began to reconsider the less conventional avenues of healing.

Wise Alternatives had been in operation long before I'd moved to Thornton, so its services could not have been too suspect. I paid a visit to them one snowy morning in November.

The woman behind the counter was unsettlingly gaunt. Her waist-length mane of frizzy silver hair was bound with a tangerine scarf. She wore a dress made of a fibrous purple material. Her bony fingers clunked with silver rings. The minute she heard the door chimes clang, the woman looked up at me and smiled. I was grateful to discover that I was the store's only customer, for the woman moved out from behind the counter, introduced herself as Roberta Twiss, and brashly asked me what was ailing me. I was too weary to invent a creative lie, or to even go through the pantomime of browsing.

"I have cancer," I'd told her. "I'm undergoing chemotherapy, but it doesn't seem to be working. I'm not here looking for a miracle cure, but I was hoping that ... I don't know ... that there might be *something*."

Without comment, Roberta wrapped her spindly arms around me. I am a man who keeps his emotions caged, but I confess that I found tremendous comfort in her embrace. A torrent of sobs suddenly, unexpectedly, came flooding out from some pained and neglected corner of my being. All the fear and agony and frustration I'd been accruing since my general physician gave me my grim diagnosis was released. After a few moments, I apologized and shamefully wiped the tears from my flushed cheeks. Roberta refused to hear any apologies, claiming instead that I had just made my first step toward recovery.

I spent the better part of that morning discussing the variety of methods that Roberta claimed to have been effective on cancer patients. I ended up leaving the store with several books, four different herbal teas, a bottle of zinc tablets ... and a questionnaire. The last item was one of the unique services Wise Alternatives performed for the public. Roberta collected information about an individual's medical history, as well as their opinions on acupuncture, raw foods, swimming with dolphins, etc. From this she would refer customers to any number of specialists that she felt would be the most complimentary to each patient.

Over the ensuing days I discovered that the herbal teas were utter swill, and that the zinc tablets were useless. But after my next chemo session rendered me unable to do anything but sleep and vomit, I vowed to fill-out and submit the questionnaire. There simply had to be a better method.

Once I had recovered from the chemotherapy I returned to Wise Alternatives.

The questionnaire was, overall, very straightforward: inquiries about the nature of my illness, how long I'd been afflicted with it, how it had impacted my appetite, my energy-level, my libido. The only question that caused me to raise an eyebrow concerned dreams. It asked me to offer my personal definition of what dreams were (This one I declined to answer), and to detail what I considered to be my most vivid nocturnal vision.

It bears mentioning here that, since childhood, I have been blessed with vivid dreams. Often these were little more than strange re-imaginings of my daily life, but their clarity and their intricate detail made each one very memorable upon waking. Had I been more ambitious, I would have probably recorded them in a journal. Since I hadn't, many of my reveries had dissolved in my memory like grains of sugar in an ocean of time. But, like most people, my mind had retained a handful of my more vividly bizarre fantasies, one of which I recounted in the questionnaire:

'It begins inside a large kitchen. Although the room; and the house in general; is unfamiliar to me, I do know that I am staying there on some kind of vacation. (Or "Rest period," as my dream-self whispers.) The kitchen floor is tiled with squares of black and white linoleum. Two large pillars (one black, one white) stand against the far wall, on either side of a slit-like rectangular window. Through this tiny band of glass shines a milky luminescence. At first I presume this to be moonlight, but when I crouch to examine it more closely I realize it is artificial; some kind of electrical light with an indirect source. It shimmers all about me, layering the kitchen with lanky shadows and opaque slabs of shadow and shadows that move like wraiths. I take a moment to study the black and white pillars and realize that they are refrigerators. I reach for the gleaming chrome handle of the white pillar and pull the curved door open. Inside I discover a mound of stuffed toys; bears, rabbits, puppies, cats.

"My daughter would like these," I say to myself (in the dream I was, apparently, a father). I reach in to pull one of the animals from the crammed shelves. The teddy bear feels like a wet sponge in my hand. Brackish water sluices through my fingers. The smell of rotted fabric fills my nostrils. Repulsed, I drop the toy into the foul puddle that has spilled on the floor. I shut the door of the white pillar and step over to the black one. This one, I discover, has no handle.

"You have to will it open," I say aloud. I then attempt to do just that; pressing my fingers against my temples: a gesture of extreme concentration.

The door must have vanished, for when I opened my eyes I found myself staring into a tank of shimmering silver, like liquid mercury, only much more translucent. Within the gleaming fluid swim odd shapes. Almost perfectly geometric in design (hexagons, dodecahedrons, etc.) but they are organic; fleshy.

Just then a voice calls out from behind me:

"TRRRRRRIIICKORRRTRRRREAT!!!!!"

The voice is tinny, laden with static. It is reminiscent of an announcer on an un-tuned radio.

I turn around to see a small black lump, approximately one-foot tall He or she is dressed in a conical hat and gown of black fabric.

"TRRRRRRIIIICKORRRRTRRRREEEEAT!" the lump repeats.

'My darling daughter,' I think to myself. I reach down and playfully removed her witch's hat by the tip. Tossing it aside, I bend down to kiss my tiny witch-

daughter on the head.

A bloated, grey face reclines to glare up at me. Its skin is horribly withered. Despite its desiccated state, its cheeks were unhealthily puffy. The creature's eyes are totally obscured by those pillows of flesh. Several gooey strands of saliva dangle from the thing's lower lip.

"IAMYOU," it says. As if on cue, the black witch's gown slides free from the round little body. The torso is compressed; more akin to the body of an obese old man than a child. Folds of grey cellulite hang over his (?) genitalia. "IAMYOU," it repeats as it reaches one of its stubby claw-like hands up to me. The thing's mouth does not seem to move in concert with the words it is speaking. I stagger back, my eyes welling up with tears of shock.

"IAMYOUIAMYOUIAMYOUYOUYOUYOUYOUYOUYOUYOU" Just then something latches itself on to the back of my head. A short, sharp shock rattles my brain. Agony shoots down the length of my spine. I shriek, my arms reaching blindly for the parasite that seems to be burrowing into the back of my head. My fingers manage to find the leeching thing and wrenches it free. I bring it into the light. It looks to be one of the geometric shapes from inside the black pillar, but it is composed entirely of what feels like human hair. A russet-coloured fluid dribbles down from a large, fleshy orifice that is blinking from inside the mass of angled hair. I reach into the pulsing hole, searching for something. What I find buried in the hair is the same dwarfish face as my "daughter."

"IAMYOU!" the face screams. Then everything vanishes in a blinding blaze of white light, and I wake up in my own bed, trembling and sweat- drenched.

*　　*　　*

When Roberta came to open Wise Alternatives the following morning she found me there waiting for her. I apologized for intruding and told her that I was very anxious to submit my questionnaire. She encouraged me to follow her inside. We entered the unlit shop and she immediately asked for the manila envelope I had tucked under my arm. When I handed it to her she tore it open and began reading its contents by the sunlight that was filtering through the shop's murky windows.

"My dream entry is a little wordy," I warned. Roberta skimmed over the three pages of legal paper upon which I had scrawled the details of my house dream. She pressed a bulbous knuckle to her lips and nodded slightly.

"I think I know just the man that can help you," she whispered. I could be mistaken, but I detected a slight quaver in her voice, as of one on the verge of tears. "His name is Benjamin Keep. But we all call him Professor; a term of endearment and respect, you understand. I think he'll be very interested in you. Dreams and sleep are what he specializes in. I'll pass this account on to him today and one of his representatives will be in touch with you very soon."

Several days passed without word. Then one afternoon I was startled from a much-needed nap by the sound of my phone ringing. I answered it and a very soft female voice asked for me by name.

"This is he," I said.

"I'm calling on behalf of Benjamin Keep," the woman said. Her voice was as soft as cream. "Professor Keep had the opportunity to review your questionnaire and he is confident he can help you. Tell me, are you well enough to venture out of your home?"

I told her that I was, but only for brief periods.

"Excellent. In that case I would like to book you for an appointment as soon as possible. Are you free this coming Wednesday evening, say, at around nine p.m.?"

"Nine? Why so late?" I asked. The woman hesitated before responding.

"Sleep is a key element to Professor Keep's method of therapy," she explained, "so a number of his clients come in for night sessions. It's much more convenient for them. It will all make sense to you once you've had a chance to meet with the Professor. Does Wednesday work for you?"

I told her that was fine.

The next day I stopped into Wise Alternatives, and when I told Roberta about my appointment she was irritatingly enthusiastic.

"Oh, you are just going to *love* Professor Keep," she gushed. "He's a brilliant man; a genuine miracle-worker."

I thanked Roberta for putting me in touch with him, though there was a part of me that was unsure as to whether I should have …

*   *   *

I moved off the dirt road and climbed the tiny wooden steps, listening to the icy tinkle of the wind chimes that dangled above the front door of the narrow house. A small scrap of paper was taped to the screen door. PLEASE RING BELL, it read. I followed the written command and a moment later the heavy wooden door was pulled back from its frame, revealing a slender grey silhouette.

"Yes?" The voice confirmed that the silhouette was that of a young woman, most likely the one I'd spoken to on the phone.

"I have an appointment with Benjamin Keep."

The woman asked for my name and I gave it to her.

"Yes, of course. The Professor's spoken of you." ('Professor' was obviously a widely-used term of endearment for the master of the house.) The woman pushed the screen door open and gestured for me to enter.

I slipped into the cold foyer. The walls were painted an odd shade of blue; one that I can only call an imitation blue; a crude, unnatural colour. The bare wood floor was marred with gouges and was badly in need of scrubbing. The chilly air was also slightly stale, lending the foyer the atmosphere of a basement in mid-winter. I thought I detected a hint of tobacco smoke as well.

There were two arched doorways on either side of the tiny foyer. A third archway yawned blackly at the end of the hall; through which the hint of closed door was discernable. The architecture was like that of a honeycomb: rooms upon rooms; laid out in some hysterical yet cryptic pattern.

"The Professor is in the sitting room here," the woman said as she passed me to enter the last archway on my right. The woman was very thin, almost too much so, but her face was uncommonly pretty.

I followed her through the doorway and into a sparsely furnished room, illuminated by a standing lamp that cast its jaundiced glow upon the elderly man that was seated in an armchair that was upholstered in a cheap green vinyl. I recognized the papers that the old man had balanced on his lap as my Wise Alternatives questionnaire.

"Welcome," said a mechanized voice. The similarity between this voice and the voice of the dwarf-thing in my dream was so certain that for a moment I actually felt faint. "I am Benjamin Keep," the voice continued. I then noticed that the reason his voice sounded so artificial was that he required the use of an artificial voice-box; a metal device that jutted from Keep's trachea. "I'm very glad you were able to join us this evening. How are you feeling?"

"I'm actually a bit tired from the walk over here," I replied.

"Of course, of course. Well, if you would like we can discuss a bit about what we do here, which I'm sure Theresa told you over the phone involves sleep- and dream-therapy. And then we can put you in our Sleep Chamber for your first session, which would also give you a chance to rest."

"That seems fine to me."

"Excellent. Why don't you have a seat on that sofa there and we can begin."

I sat down and Keep leaned forward in his chair. He too was almost skeletal in appearance. He was lantern-jawed, and his head was capped with a sweep of white hair that looked as though it would be as soft as the bristles of a fine paintbrush. Keep then began a lengthy explanation of his personal philosophy.

I don't know whether it was the alien-ness of Keep's mechanically-enhanced voice, my poor health and exhaustion, or the oddness of the whole situation; but whatever the reason I can recall almost nothing of Keep's lecture. I seem to remember him mentioning something about how it was necessary for one who is physically ill to create a psychic healing centre, a place that one can dream about at will and where one can undergo an internal healing process, but even this I'm not totally certain of.

My bewildered state must have become evident at some point, for Professor Keep rose from his chair and called for Theresa.

"We'd better get him into the Sleep Chamber right away," Theresa said.

The two of them escorted me out of the den, down a long hallway, and finally through a basement door. Theresa was whispering words of consolation to me, which did much to ease my natural apprehensions about what was happening.

"Careful now, mind the steps," buzzed Keep's mock-voice. The wood of the cellar steps groaned under my weight as I cautiously descended them. A waft of incredibly damp air caused me to shudder. I looked about and noticed that the basement's psychedelic illumination was in the form of a mural of stars and a full-moon that had been painted on the ceiling in gaudy, Day-glo colours. The croaking of toads and the chirping of crickets filled my ears. Like something out of a surrealist film, the entire basement had been transformed into a marshland. The room was half-filled with stagnant water. Artificial bulrushes and lily pads authenticated the environment. A fog of dry ice cascaded lazily across the water, obscuring the room's dimensions, thus making the area seem boundless.

From the stairway I was able to see a handful of people, each floating on their own inflatable raft, which were tethered to the cement walls. The people bobbed and slid gently upon the foul pool. Their motionlessness conveyed a deep contentment.

"What is …," I began.

"Please be as quiet as you can," Theresa whispered. "This is our Sleep Chamber; a controlled environment used for dream therapy. There are five other patients sleeping down here. Now, just hold onto the railing for a moment and I'll fetch you a raft."

Like a fool I stood and watched while Theresa pulled an inflatable raft from the shadows. She pulled it to the bottom of the stairway and assisted me in lying down upon it. Despite some feeble protesting, I soon found myself floating within this strange vault.

"Now just relax," Theresa whispered. "The Professor and I will be retiring upstairs. We no longer need the stimulus of the room to reach the Sanctuary. Don't worry, you'll will meet up with us soon enough. Just rest."

The fake nocturnal environment had a definite affect on me. A soft and beautiful exhaustion overcame me, and within moments I was lost in dreaming.

The dream began with my emerging from the bottom of a swamp. I pushed my way through the reeds and onto the muddy shore. A full moon shone down, dappling all things with ghostly phosphorescence. I was very cold and hungry. A pathway led from the swampy ravine and up a great hill. I noticed a fire burning at the top of the hill, its flames all weepy and bright in the night.

I moved up the hill with ease, feeling tremendously energetic. I no longer felt the cold or dampness, though my hunger remained. When I reached the top of the hill I saw a man and a woman tossing what looked to be large bundles of linen onto the pyre. The woman turned and I immediately recognized her as Theresa.

"That was very fast," she exclaimed.

The man, who I now knew was Professor Keep, turned to face me.

"I had an inkling that you were a bit of a prodigy for this," he said. His voice was strong and clear. His physique was also noticeably burlier. "Yes, I am much different in dreaming, as are you. You can probably feel that your cancer doesn't afflict you here. The key is to bring some of this health back with you into the waking world."

"What is this place?" I asked.

"A form of hospice," Keep replied, "a sanctuary; a place where people can rest and heal themselves."

"What are you burning?"

A heavy stench gushed out from the flames.

"Refuse," Theresa replied. "Come inside. Annie is already there. The others should hopefully be along soon."

I turned to see a massive Colonial-style mansion standing just a few feet from where I was standing. Its white exterior practically glowed in the semi-darkness of the dream world. The three of us moved across the lawn and into the house. Its interior was cosily furnished. No lights were on, but the moonlight lit each room amply. A woman (one I recognized from Keep's basement marsh) sat meditating inside the living room.

"Each does his or her own thing," Keep explained.

"Why the swamp? Both here and in your ... your real house; a swamp. Why?"

"The marsh represents a wonderful transitory state," Keep explained, "it is neither solid land nor flowing water. It's an in-between place, and all humans know this, albeit subconsciously. So, lying in a swamp-like room opens your mind, makes you receptive."

"Receptive to this place?"

"And other things."

I then noticed something scuttling across the floor behind Keep.

"What was that?" I asked. The complacency I'd been feeling was quickly draining. A cold, sickening dread was its usurper.

"He saw it!" Theresa exclaimed. "I told you when we reviewed his dream journal that he was too attuned ..."

"HUSH!" shouted Keep.

I turned my gaze to the living room. My insides turned to water once I saw the little grey creature crawling upon the meditating woman, who, incredibly, seemed oblivious to the molestations of the rotting, dwarf-like thing. It pried the woman's jaws open to a preposterous degree.

"What is it doing?" I cried.

Yet somehow I knew.

Like a dream within a dream, I then remembered the first time I had seen this very creature; in that distant nightmare from my youth. And suddenly all the high strangeness of my nightmare was scraped away and the dream's true import became glaringly apparent.

It was an omen, a premonition.

Keep was not providing the sick with an entry into an astral paradise; he was using them to provide entry for the twisted things that no longer wished to be confined to the realm of dark dreams.

"iamyou ..." I muttered. And I suddenly knew to whirl around. I did so just in time to escape the clawing grasp of the creature that was attempting to tear its stubby hooks into the back of my head. Its arm flailed at me from between the banister spokes of the large staircase.

"We have to keep him here," Theresa said.

"Wait," Keep said to me as I shuffled back from him. "You of all people can appreciate what we are doing here. Your body is sick and weak, and that means that, like the swamp, you're in a state of transition. Just let a few of them through and you can live on. They'll eat your cancer, just as they did mine. They'll sustain you for as long as you wish. They need us as much as we need them. All you'd have to do is be a conduit for them to pass through."

Professor Keep reached for me, but I was already falling, falling ...

I must have tumbled off of my raft and into the frigid water of Keep's basement marsh. I was so weak I could barely right myself in the waist-high pool. I pushed my through the bulrushes and the reeds on my way to the basement stairs. Something in my peripheral vision twitched. I heard a soft splash of water. I turned to my right. I spotted Annie slung over her raft, her spindly limbs dragging in the water like oars. Her head was reclined over the edge of the narrow raft, and something was struggling to free itself from her mouth. The Day-glo constellation only allowed me to see a hint of the bloated, slug-like head that was squirming to dislodge itself from the woman's cracked jaws. If I'd had the strength I would have drowned the creature, but I was just able to pull myself up the stairs and out the basement door.

Someone grabbed me the instant I emerged from the archway.

"Theresa!" shouted Keep, though his voice was scarcely louder than a whisper. He wrapped his dry hands around my throat. Some deep-seated instinct for survival gave me a sudden surge of energy, for I managed to throw the old man off me. I heard him tumble backward down the basement stairs. The sickening thudding noises were immediately followed by a splash.

Theresa came running toward me, her eyes wide and positively feral. I am convinced she would have murdered me right there at the top of the stairs had she not seen Professor Keep fall down into the cellar swamp.

She tore down the stairs, screaming Keep's name over and over. I heard her dragging the water with her arms. Perhaps the old man was lying unconscious at the bottom of the fetid pool. Perhaps he had broken his neck during the fall. I cared little either way. Seizing the opportunity, I moved as quickly as my weakened state would allow me to. My heart felt as though it were about to burst. I could hear Theresa screaming. Any second now she would find Keep and would come after me, to prevent me from ever leaving this house and telling the world what I had learned.

An impossible distance seemed to stand between me and the front door. I staggered along the hall. Behind me I could hear the heavy footfalls of someone storming up the cellar stairs.

My fingers fumbled with the deadbolt locks. At last they gave way. I could still hear Theresa shrieking as I pushed my way out of the house and into the foggy night.

I staggered along the streets, howling like a wounded animal; it was the only sound I could muster. A porch light shone like a beacon from one of the houses on the beach strip. I stumbled up their driveway. I slapped my hand upon their front window again and again, until a great darkness swallowed me whole.

*   *   *

I awoke to find myself in a hospital bed. The people whose house I had run to called 911 and I was immediately admitted.

There were many questions posed to me over the ensuing two days. But I will take the liberty of abbreviating the outcome of my experience with Professor Keep:

The doctors believed that I'd hallucinated the entire experience. My illness, you see; it plays havoc with the mind. After a thorough examination the doctors discovered that, in addition to my inoperable cancer of the stomach, recent X-rays revealed I had now developed an abnormal cell growth in my cerebellum. I was not at all surprised. I had closed the gate before my own little aberration had fully developed. Its vestiges were left in me to fester.

The Keep house burned to the ground the night after I'd escaped. The newspaper described the incident as occurring to "a derelict house" that was probably burned by thrill-seeking youths. Apparently no one was harmed.

Once I was released from the hospital I immediately set out to corroborate my story with Roberta Twiss. Wise Alternatives had closed its doors. Within a matter of days the shop's inventory, along with its proprietor, had disappeared into the night. I am quite certain that this group of conspirators will be setting up operations in some distant town where they can resume executing their twisted little plan.

As for myself: the cancer is spreading at a rapid rate. I am rarely able to leave my bed. The worst part of the affliction isn't the pain or my own impending doom; it is the fact that I am moving toward a horribly uncertain fate. I know that when my body shuts down I will have no hospice to seek refuge in. For all its monstrosities, at least Keep's sanctuary provided solitude, provided *life*, regardless of how ugly.

These are mad thoughts, to be sure. But one cannot help but long for the comforts of Hell when they're standing at the edge of oblivion.

"Well, it's official," Dennis Combs announced, tossing the torn envelope onto the table, "I'm married to a felon. I always knew there was something shady about you."

Beth felt herself blushing as she dragged the envelope back.

"I told you," she began, "it was an honest mistake, an accident. I saw the handwritten envelope and just assumed that Gloria had replied to the letter I sent her at Thanksgiving. I didn't know the letter was for Mr. Branch until *after* I'd opened it."

"Opened the envelope and *read* part of the letter inside. That's a crime." Dennis winked at her then reached for the carafe of coffee that sat cooling on the table between them. The damp November morning made it apparent that the retired couple's daily breakfasts on the screened-in sun porch were numbered until next Spring.

"OK, I confess that I read a little more than I should have, but even you have to admit that the prospect of learning more about what goes on inside that house over there is very tempting." Beth scooped some grapefruit from the rind, shot a sideward glance at the house across the road, and then added "After all, I'm only human."

The nearby house was narrow and bore a cheap white clapboard façade and a patina-scarred trim of hunter green. Several grime-fogged windows, whose curtains seemed to be forever drawn, shimmered weakly under the cold sun. The tarmac roof bowed sadly beneath an unseen weight. Were it not for the fact that a local landscaping company were paid to sporadically tend to the property, the reclusive Mr. Branch's yard would have surely been a jungle.

Dennis glanced again at the envelope, the inside of which was darkened with a swirling grey pattern to keep its contents hidden. He lighted a cigarette with his dented Zippo and said, "The postmark is from six months ago. Did you notice that? This letter must've been sitting in the dead letter office for quite a while before it was accidentally put in our P.O. Box." After a lengthy pause Dennis asked, "So was it worth reading?"

"Hmm?" Beth said, breaking her trance with the neglected property.

"The letter, was there anything juicy in it?"

Beth slid the sheets from their hiding place beneath her napkin. The letter was eight pages in length. The heavy-bond sheets were the colour of curdled milk and bore the faded grey-ink scarring of a manual typewriter. The numerous dollops of White-Out evidenced the fact that the author had poor typing skills. The letter had been crisply folded-over twice and hosted a faint fragrance of sandalwood.

"Well, there are a lot of references to Qabalah," Beth said.

"To what?"

"Qabalah. It's a kind of ancient mystical puzzle, I think. Rabbis are trained in it."

"I didn't know Branch was Jewish."

"You don't have to be Jewish to study Qabalah, Dennis. It's actually very *en vogue* with celebrities these days."

Dennis huffed. He tugged one corner of the letter down to glance at the hand-drawn diagram of circles interconnected by an intricate network of lines. The notes which had been jotted all around the diagram were barely legible; and those that Dennis could make out were meaningless. He read:

> *'Here, lurking below Tiphereth, is the Doorway to Daath (Death?). The hidden sephirah, the cosmic masque, the Gate to the Abyss. When opened, Daath releases the preeval lifewave, which forever alters those that attune their minds to its strange frequency ...'*

"A crock," he said, downing the dregs of coffee from his mug. "Put the letter back in the envelope. I'll take it across the street and explain things to Mr. Branch."

"Oh, please don't," Beth pleaded, "I'm so embarrassed. Couldn't you just slide it under his door or something?"

"Fine, fine, but I'm going now. I want to get those leaves raked up before it rains."

Beth tented her fingers before her face, whose contours had softened and grown sallow with time. She peered out over the rim of her bifocals to watch her husband marching purposefully across the foliage-carpeted lawn toward the dim house across the road.

Dennis' knock on the front door resounded through the hollows of the Branch house. He tried to rouse its occupant twice more before finally leaning toward the living room window and peering through it. The off-white curtains hanging behind the glass were stained with marrow-yellow blotches. Sheer as the draperies were, they still managed to successfully conceal most of the house's interior. Through a worn patch a thin slice of the living room floor was visible.

A small coffee table stood upon a tattered spiral-pattern throw-rug. The table bore what looked to be a glass candy dish, piled high with dust-enrobed sweets. A small loveseat, upholstered in ugly brocade fabric, sat near the kitchen archway. The glow that reached the kitchen must have been filtered through another dirty white curtain, for it was meek and sickly. Dennis pulled himself back and decided to make a quick check of the rear of the house.

The nightly clawing of raccoons and stray cats had frayed the screen of Mr. Branch's backdoor. The animals must have been quite feral … and large. Dennis noticed sizeable gouges in the inner wooden door as well. He cupped his hands on either side of his face and squinted to see through the window. A mop stood propped against an antiquated refrigerator. A brown amoeba of spilt tea was visible on the kitchen floor, along with the teethy shards of a shattered china cup. Food-encrusted dishes were piled in the basin. The door of one of the hanging cupboards hung halfway open, as did the door leading to the basement. A wedge of dense shadow stood firm between the frame and the half-open basement door.

Dennis found himself wondering if the basement door being left ajar was a gesture of invitation, perhaps from Mr. Branch, perhaps from something else altogether.

When his knock went unanswered yet again, Dennis returned to the front of the house and placed the letter between the outer and inner doors. He resisted the temptation to glance back at the house once he'd crossed the road. Frigid glass eyes seemed to be caressing the flesh between his shoulder blades. Even after he was safely back on his own property and was occupying himself by raking soggy leaves into tidy mounds, Dennis could not bring himself to face the menacing property.

*   *   *

When Beth saw Dennis jogging back toward the house she quickly re-concealed the page of Branch's letter that she had secreted from her husband. Much to her frustration, Beth discovered that the page she'd taken was the penultimate, not the final, sheet. It read:

> 'In your letter to me you claimed that you only wrote Beneath the House of Life *to teach children not to be afraid of the dark. And I think you were being honest. Now I'm being honest by saying that although this might have been your conscious reason for writing and illustrating this story, your subconscious had altogether different reasons for providing you with those images.*
>
> *'Your images and descriptions are so bloody specific: the front porch of Mr. Junktongue's old house having a statue of a Queen seated upon Her throne is a blatant reference to Malkuth; the tenth sephera, the gate to the Tree of Life.*
>
> *'The connections go on from there; your placement of the beautiful daughter's 'bedroom of emerald' (Netzach), the fact*

that you called the son 'strangely mannered' and 'odd-looking', hiding in his 'russet-coloured room' until he finally escaped down into the cellar to hide from life. This is the secret formula of Hod, the Hermaphrodite who sunk down below Tiphareth, down through the Gates of Daath that hide beneath the Tree (or, to use your preferred term, 'House') of Life. This is the most disturbing aspect of your book: You didn't teach the wonders of Qabalah, instead you chose to show the seamy side, the dark side, of this mystical model.

'You have crafted an ideal fable to illustrate the transmutation of the body. This occurs when we open ourselves up to the primeval past that exists in our subconscious. Do you fully understand the import of what you have done? This formula is terrifying proof that Thought can alter matter to a grotesque degree. Certain Words of Power call up the hideous powers that were cast out of this universe and into a second universe. The unclean, incomplete, illogical universe. This is the universe where all our nightmares come from. It is the source of all our Hell myths.

Therefore I MUST ask you: Why did you feel the need to pass on this monstrous magic to children, Mr. Branch?

Beth slid the sheet into her pants pocket and began a pantomime of tidying the living room. Keeping secrets from her spouse wasn't something she enjoyed doing, but she knew how Dennis would react if he discovered that she'd not only read Mr. Branch's letter, but had kept a portion of it for her own study. Dennis did not possess her inquisitive nature, her passion for puzzles and cryptic things. Qabalistic philosophy was too complicated for her to grasp in one reading, and even with the notes she'd taken, Beth was still unable to appreciate the import and nuance of terms like 'the House of Life' or 'Physical Reversion'. Fortunately she had been insightful enough to record a title which, though never quoted from, was mentioned numerous times: *Beneath the House of Life*. Beth thought about the book as she washed and put away the morning's dishes.

When her peripheral vision passed the stack of unread novels from the public library in Hemmingford, Beth conjured a plan.

She tossed on her coat and went out to the yard, which was perfumed with the earthy smell of burning leaves.

"Dennis?" she called.

Her husband jolted from the sound of her voice.

"Jesus God, woman," he gasped, half-chuckling, "you trying to give me a coronary?"

"Of course not," she replied. "What's with the trash bag?"

"I found *another* dead squirrel on the lawn; mangled all to hell."

"Don't show me, please."

"You know, for a house with so few cars driving past we sure do get a lot of road kill here."

"Are you going to need the truck this afternoon?" Beth asked.

"No. Why?"

"I was going to return these to the library, then get something nice from the supermarket for supper."

Dennis nodded. "Drive carefully."

He turned back to the crackling mound. Through the ribbons of blue-grey smoke Dennis saw the front door of Mr. Branch's house slowly shutting. For a moment he thought about racing across the road and hammering on the front door, but then realized how ridiculous that would've been. Perhaps Branch had just gotten home from a walk, or a vacation. A trip would explain why he'd not been seen in town lately, and why his home was in such a state. He stood with the rake in his fist, waving at Beth as she backed the truck onto the road and drove away.

Beth's search for Qabalistic material in the library's computer system was successful, linking her keyword with alternate spellings of Kabbalah and Cabala, as well as with Mysticism and Gematria. Beth wandered to the appropriate section and a legion of triangulated eyes, pentagrams, hexagrams, and astrological symbols all vied for her attention from the rows of book spines.

She found one (*Beginner's Qabalah*) which seemed to suit her needs. She used the book's index to cross-reference any of the terms she remembered from Mr. Branch's letter.

'Daath' was mentioned several times in the chapter entitled 'Deep Qabalah.' Beth turned to the appropriate chapter and scanned the pages until she came upon the following passage:

'Though little information exists, in either Rabbinical or the less formal Cabalistic writings, there are still a few surviving myths about the mysterious 'false sephirah' known as Daath. Daath is a trapdoor that reputedly opens unto the dreaded abyss of the failed creation. Beyond this 'hidden' or 'false' sephirah there dwells all manner of hideous remnants from the pre-human universes. They are the unwanted leavings of our universe that were cast into the pit by God, the Creator. Here, underneath the Tree of Life, there lurk dark life-forms. Just as there are many humans striving to climb the Tree and reach

116

the Godhead, there are others who wish to descend into the murkiest depths, to commune with its foul denizens. These barbarous energies cannot properly be called 'evil', for their intentions are not necessarily malevolent or destructive, but they are unclean and wholly alien to ordinary human consciousness. The abyss beyond Daath is unlike the phenomenal universe of growth, life and light. Daath is a noumenal, cold and barren place. A realm where one regresses into grotesque parodies of life, devolving until they reach the very sentient slime from which all protein life was moulded at the dawn of time. If the traditional Qabalistic Tree of Life can be thought of as the Mind of God, the Creator, then the substratum of Daath can be viewed as His subconscious.'

Beth closed the cover and moved to the checkout, ensuring that the book's title was hidden against her chest.

When the librarian asked Beth if she'd found everything she was looking for, by rote Beth said yes.

"Actually, no," she added, suddenly remembering another phrase from the mysterious letter. "I was wondering about something called *Beneath the House of Life*."

The librarian tapped the title into the keyboard. After a moment she said, "We actually have a children's book *Beneath the House of Life* by T. M. Branch down in our storage area; that's where we put all the books that have been pulled from circulation due to lack of activity."

"Is there any way I could sign it out?" Beth asked.

The librarian frowned. "Well, I suppose, but I'd have to have one of our part-timers go through all the boxes downstairs."

"Would you mind? I hate to ask, but it's important."

The librarian offered Beth an expression that was equal parts smile and sneer. "It might take a while," she said.

"I don't mind waiting."

Half an hour later a young man whose khakis and sweater bore telltale patches of dirt and a few tufts of cobweb presented Beth with a slender hardbound volume. The dust jacket was tattered and faded beneath its Mylar sleeve. A vein-like white crease sliced through the muted night colours of the cover illustration, which depicted a young boy standing before a grotesquely thin, tall house whose many rooms were unlit, except for the front door, which shone with a yellowish light. A dark figure was visible inside the glowing archway.

Beneath the House of Life,
A Fable
Written & Illustrated by T. M. Branch

Beth checked the books out and departed.

During the homeward drive Beth felt the book pulling at her. It felt as though some force was reaching out from the book's musty leaves to taunt Beth's imagination.

She hid the book under her coat when she entered the house. After stashing the volume in the upstairs bedroom, Beth went downstairs to try and occupy her mind with the preparation of dinner.

Beth was so eager to delve into Branch's book that was barely able to sit still, let alone eat the steak she'd broiled. After the kitchen was cleaned, Beth announced that she was going to head off to bed early to read. Dennis stifled his pleasure at hearing this and muttered something about sitting out on the porch for a while.

Beth knew she would have a good hour or two of uninterrupted study. She went upstairs and retrieved her volumes with an almost embarrassing degree of excitement.

> *'Nevertown was a town with a shortage of lore,'* Branch's
> fable began, *'nothing really ever happened in Nevertown.*
> *Most of its residents did not even know each other by name.*
> *Instead they made up nicknames to describe one another.*
> *There was Scrawny Bookworm, Nevertown's elderly librarian;*
> *and Bloato, the rotund bread baker who always seemed to be*
> *smiling; and many others.*
>
> *'But there was one man in Nevertown that was almost never*
> *seen. He was an old man who lived in the tall house on a*
> *dead-end lane. Everyone in Nevertown called this old man*
> *Junktongue, not because he chewed garbage but because in*
> *olden times he was always, Always, ALWAYS talking rubbish*
> *and nonsense.*
>
> *'The kids in town had been told that old Junktongue had*
> *been the schoolmaster until the parents in Nevertown, who'd*
> *grown tired of his teaching non-stop nonsense, burned his*
> *schoolhouse down. Junktongue refused to leave Nevertown. He*
> *built a crazy house for himself at the end of a shady lane and*
> *never left it. Junktongue hid for many years, plotting his*
> *revenge against Nevertown. He stayed inside with his mad*
> *thoughts. To this day the Nevertown kids were frightened that*
> *Junktongue would one day burst out his lopsided front door*

and hatch his mad revenge on them …'

Beth winced at the gruesome tale. She read on as the fable told of a brave Nevertown boy who sought to prove that Junktongue was just a misunderstood hermit, but once he ventured out to *'that teetering old mansion, which Junktongue had named Leanloom,'* he was led on a guided tour through the old man's shadow-filled madhouse, and told about how Leanloom was designed to a very specific task, the secret of which could be found in the basement. Junktongue had figured out a way to bring some friends in to visit from far outside of Nevertown.

By the time Beth reached the finale of the young protagonist's tour through Junktongue's crooked home she found herself short of breath. To her crushing disappointment, Beth discovered that the final page of the story had been torn from the book.

Flipping back to the illustration that depicted the Nevertown boy descending the tiny stairway into Junktongue's cellar, Beth rubbed the corner of the page between her thumb and forefinger in the hope that the sheets were stuck together. But the jagged tear that ran along the book's spine evidenced that Beth was forced to merely speculate as to the nature of the secret beneath Junktongue's house of life.

Though there was nothing overtly offensive in the narrative itself, Beth nonetheless found Branch's fable to be … unsanitary, for youthful minds. Had she been a mother she certainly would never had let her children read such a thing.

Beth reached over to collect *Beginner's Qabalah* and the absconded page of Branch's letter. She failed to see the strong Qabalistic undercurrent in Branch's book until she took a note pad and began jotting down her own observations of *Beneath the House of Life* in comparison to the information presented in *Beginner's Qabalah*. An hour and eleven hand-scribbled pages later, Beth felt simultaneously elated and exhausted. Her puzzle-hungry mind had struck gold with this obscure thread of inquiry. She flipped back through her notes and was amazed that Branch had *not* used the Tree of Life or Qabalistic philosophy as the basis for his fable. Every colour depicted in Leanloom, every name mentioned by Junktongue, every hallway he led the Nevertown boy through, corresponded perfectly with this mystical model for the universe and all its complex workings. Beth had learned more about Qabalah by this slender children's book than she probably would have by any other means of education. What was even more chilling was the possibility that Branch might've injected the tale with some autobiographical tidbits; he was certainly this town's version of Junktongue in the sense that he was reclusive to the point of being whispered about in near-mythical manner by the locals.

If only she could discover how the story ended.

Beth knew from her research that the Tree of Life was a model for the universe; and emanation of the Divine, the Godhead. *The universe is Thought; the dream of the Godhead,'* the primer explained. All of the ten sephirah (spheres) were particular aspects of the great Thought, and all ten aspects form the perfect universe. *Beginner's Qabalah* argued that any thought, any action, any form can be neatly assigned into one of the sephirah, and each one also holds a shard of the great Thought. All things are connected, all are born of God. This was hardly a unique thought, Beth knew, but the chapter 'Deep Qabalah' nagged at her mind.

> 'Some believe there is an eleventh sephirah. A hidden, false sephirah. A gateway to the abyss of all that is unclean and unbidden.'

She thought of Junktongue egging the Nevertown boy to open the mouldy cellar door, to peer into the dark heart of his House of Life.

Beth's eyes were stinging from overstrain. Her shoulders felt stiff. She slid her books and notepad under the bed and switched off the light. Gradually she drifted off to sleep by the creaking sound of Dennis rocking in the porch swing.

*   *   *

In the colder seasons Dennis always kept a six-pack in a large plastic bucket on the sun porch. Hidden beneath a bundle of old paint rags, the stashed beer was always well hidden from Beth and naturally chilled by the air. Dennis had convinced himself that this form of refrigeration improved the flavour of the beer. He popped the tab on one of the cans and drank, all the while eyeing the Branch property.

As he was lighting his last cigarette, Dennis wondered if he'd really witnessed the door closing earlier today or whether it was mental trickery. Of course the best way to determine which was true would be to sneak back over there and see if the letter was still resting between the front doors. Dennis decided he would do just that, but not now. He hadn't enough alcohol-fuelled bravado just yet. So Dennis sat and drank and listened to the muted sounds of the night. The light from Beth's window cast a glowing square upon the front lawn. But his wife must have grown weary of reading and of waiting, for she switched the light off, plunging him into utter darkness.

Dennis decided that bed sounded good. Better than good; wonderful, essential. But the distance between the sun porch and the bedroom seemed insurmountable in his weary, drunken state. Besides, he still wanted to check

on Branch's letter. He would do both once he took a moment to rest his
eyes ...

A warbled voice gradually roused him. Assuming he'd once again fallen
asleep with the TV on, Dennis reached for the remote, but suddenly
remembered where he was. Dennis experienced a jarring shudder. His limbs
ached from shivering. He opened his eyes and saw the moon and the pitch-
silhouettes of trees. Dennis wondered how long he'd been asleep. He pinched
the flesh between his eyes and groaned. His yawning distorted the chattering
voice even further. But of course there was no television set on the sun porch,
and the small transistor he listened to the ballgames on was switched off. He
stilled himself and listened.

A shadow shifted. There was the sudden whisking sound of something
brushing past the screen wall of the sun porch. Dennis' head refused to
turn. Instead he stole a sidelong glimpse of the thing that clung to the
latticework.

The raccoon skittered to and fro, its head jutting out to study the old man
in the mesh cage. Dennis sighed with relief and stood. The raccoon swatted
one of its large claws against the screen and held it there. The banging sound
startled Dennis, who told the creature in a harsh whisper to shoo.

But raccoons cannot speak, nor do they have simian-like hands, or leathery
webbing stretched between their elongated fingers; webbing that glistens in
the moonlight with some thick secretion. As Dennis' eyes grew accustomed to
the lack of light he was able to see the drawn face of the ranting thing. Its
visage was a horrible hybrid of baboon and lemur. The eyes were bright and
clear and searing. Its wide mouth rippled with every babbling word. Although
Dennis could not understand a single syllable of the creature's rant, he was
also certain that these were not mere animal grunts. It was nearly human, but
not quite. A dwarfish little mock-voice. Shrill mutters washed over Dennis
without pause or cadence or rhythm. Words, or something like words, were
being vomited out in one great spiel. Was the thing trying to communicate
with him, to pass on something it deemed to be knowledge?

Dennis heard himself shout "NO!" It was a response not to the creature's
pleadings, but to the creature itself, its very ugly presence. It was Dennis
calling to nature that this encounter, this *thing*, should not, *must* not be.

The creature hurled itself off the screen. It landed on Dennis' lawn with a
padded thump. Dennis watched with disbelieving eyes as the thing pushed
itself backward across his property. The creature seemed to be carrying itself
upon a pair of long, ropey arms which he swung backward like windmill
blades. Back and back it went, swiftly merging with the darkness, vanishing
altogether.

Still lost in slumber, Beth turned onto her side and instinctively reached her arm to Dennis' side of the bed. When she found it cold and vacant, Beth stirred, sat up and groggily called her husband's name.

A quavering voice answered, "I'm over here."

In the murk of fledgling daylight Dennis' features appeared clouded, indistinct. He was sitting in the old wooden chair by the bedroom window, a knitted afghan wrapped around his body, which seemed small and frail.

"Everything OK?" Beth mumbled.

"Fine. I have a touch of insomnia, that's all."

"Have you not been to bed all night?"

Dennis shook his head, coughed. Beth flung back the sheets and pulled her on her robe.

"Come and lay down," she said, "and I'll go downstairs to heat you up some milk. That will help you sleep."

"But it's nearly seven."

"So sleep in. You're retired, remember? It's not like you need to go anywhere. The yard work can wait."

After she brought the steaming mug in to Dennis, Beth dressed herself and went downstairs to start on the laundry.

At the cusp of the basement Beth found herself feeling uneasy. The memory of the unfinished fable flowered in her mind and, like last night, it took possession of her thoughts.

Perhaps there would be more clues in the letter ...

Dennis had returned it yesterday, but perhaps it was still there. Beth swallowed back her anxiousness, went downstairs and tried to combat her mounting curiosity with mundane chores.

It was ineffective, for in a matter of minutes Beth found herself reasoning that she would just read the letter once and then put it back exactly where she'd found it. No one would be the wiser.

After slipping upstairs to ensure that Dennis was asleep, Beth donned her boots and coat and crept quietly out the front door.

Dennis' brief slumber was shattered when the drooping, baboon-like mask lunged out at him from some occult zone of the dream realm. He could clearly see the creature's dripping fangs, the topaz-glint of its wide eyes; could hear the panicked mutter of its teachings ...

Dennis laid and listened to his heart hammering inside his chest. His body ached with exhaustion, yet he knew that sleep would unobtainable. He rose and drew himself a warm bath. Sinking into the steaming water felt good. He soaked and smoked two cigarettes in succession.

That thing in the night seemed to have been heading back to Branch's house. Dennis was certain of it. What *was* Branch up to inside that house? Was he even alive? Dennis wracked his brain in an attempt to recall the last time he'd actually seen the spindly old man. Summertime, or perhaps even earlier. He wondered if someone should be called. The sheriff's office, or even Dr. Dietz in town.

It occurred to Dennis that the best avenue was to first see if the letter he'd left between Branch's doors was still there. If it wasn't, then he could be reasonably sure that Branch was still rattling around inside that gloomy house of his. If it was there Dennis would make a few calls, just to put his mind at ease.

He towelled off and dressed warmly, for the November wind was moaning coldly just beyond the window.

As Dennis was exiting their home, Beth was returning to it. She said something about taking some dead houseplants out to the trash. Dennis announced that he was going to finish up the yard work in order to tire himself for a long nap.

Beth kissed his cheek before slipping inside the house and shutting the door.

Dennis did his best to pretend to be puttering around the yard until, through the study window, he noticed that Beth had settled down at her desk, pen in hand. He would give her a few minutes to become engrossed in her crosswords before attempting to slip away.

He felt like a child deliberately defying his mother.

A pickup truck rounded the corner just as Dennis was about to cross the road. He performed a pantomime of inspecting the oak tree in his front yard until the vehicle passed. He felt foolish for panicking, but something about the task at hand felt … improper.

The wind was bitingly cold and carried a few plump flakes of wet snow. Dennis turned the collar of his coat up. The Branch house was customarily dim and still, but this morning Dennis found these once-daunting qualities to be rather enticing. His appetite for answers had grown keener since his strange encounter with the thing on the porch.

He scaled the front steps of Branch's house as quickly and quietly as he could. Tugging the screen door open, Dennis was unsure how to react when he noticed that the letter was no longer resting between the doors. The hazy memory of Branch's front door shutting silently across the road, the shadows that slithered behind curtained windows, the scratching in the dead of night …

Dennis could rest easy. Obviously the old hermit was still skulking about somewhere.

Just to be sure, Dennis thought he'd investigate the backdoor as well.

*   *   *

Much to Beth's dismay, the final page of Branch's letter shed no further light on the whole baffling ordeal. In fact the epistle's closing page offered only two scant yet icy lines:

'I've highlighted the most powerful words from the 'harmless graffiti' that Junktongue's mutant child scribbled on the basement walls. Look closely at these words as they were printed on the final page of your storybook. They are the formula for Primordial Reversion inside the Abyss. This formula changes the telluric lifewave, rebirths the world into a world that God didn't allow to flourish. If you really do think I'm 'just projecting my own philosophies' on your book as you suggested in your letter, go ahead and light a lantern in a sub-telluric chamber and say these circled words aloud. As a matter of fact, I dare you to.'

There was no closing signature to identify the letter's author. Beth felt a little nauseous, and more than a little bewildered. Where was this noxious 'formula'? Beth splayed the sheets out on the glass-top desk and pored over every pale-inked character in search of a pattern, a code, a key.

Deflated, Beth refolded the letter and held the envelope open.

A pair of dull yellow eyes stared out at Beth from the inside of the envelope.

Beth opened the envelope wider. The envelope's shaded interior was in fact an illustration. The piece of scotch tape that held one side of the envelope together split. At first Beth winced at her accidental destruction of T. M. Branch's personal property, but with a slight tug the dried-out adhesive gave and Beth was able to unfold the envelope and discover the final page from *Beneath the House of Life.*

The blue-washed illustration depicted a cluttered basement. Beth recognized the silhouetted profile of the Nevertown boy as he reached up to her from the page. The darkness of the basement pinned him to the wooden stairway. But then Beth saw the misshapen form that was squatting down upon the young child's back. The glowing lemur-like eyes stared madly. The spit-shiny teeth were bared in either ferocity or glee, Beth could not tell which.

The basement wall in the illustration bore a number of frantic black ink circles. Certain bits graffiti were illuminated with ballpoint pen halos.

*   *   *

The first sight to greet Dennis was the back screen door dangling from the topmost hinge. The screen itself was shredded, strips of wire mesh lapped in the wind like tongues. As he approached the back steps Dennis noted that the inside door had been smashed from its frame, it lay halved upon the kitchen floor, which was now carpeted with dead leaves and other debris from the yard.

A wind pushed past Dennis and flooded the kitchen, causing the leaves to whisper, to move in vertigo.

The sound of his foot landing on the tile floor thundered through the house. A stale smell like the inside of old wooden trunk crowded Dennis' nostrils when he leaned his head (hesitantly) into the room.

"Hulloh?" he said meekly. Something cold and clammy moved down the skin of his back. Dennis shook the feeling off.

"You in here, Mr. Branch?"

The response came in the form of the sound of a door opening.

Dennis left the bright chill of the day and entered T. M. Branch's soft, grey world. A childish feeling of doing something forbidden exhilarated Dennis' aged spirit. He exited the kitchen, made his way into the living room. Unable to resist, Dennis moved to the front window and peered out at his house across the road.

The flakes that were swirling around Dennis' house made it look like a prop in a snow-globe, a replica trapped in glass and water for all to spy on. The resemblance disturbed him. Dennis looked away.

He stood for a moment, listening for any signs of movement. The usual pops, clicks and soft groans of a house settling were amplified to grotesque proportions. Dennis ran a hand over the back of his neck and found it soaked with perspiration. He became keenly aware of the fact that his bladder was full.

Dennis moved to the back door, and he would've made a hasty exit from the house had he not heard Beth cry out suddenly from beyond the basement door.

*   *   *

The first word from the storybook graffiti, if it was in fact a word, sounded ridiculous to Beth when she whispered it to only the study's four silent walls. The strange inflection was intriguing to her, and sounded more appealing when she repeated it, along with the two words that followed it. She felt her mouth curling into an amused grin.

*   *   *

Dennis did not hear Beth cry out again. He would've managed to convince himself that it was an auditory hallucination, or a bad joke, were his conscience (and his curiosity) not so potent.

He stepped onto the landing of the basement stairs. Of course the questions of how or why Beth would be down in the dank confines of Branch's basement did not matter to Dennis. His sole concern was finding her, bringing her back into the light.

Dennis could see, even with the lack of light, that the basement was unfinished. Spine-like columns of stone jutted up from the dirt floor to meet the ribcage of creaking wooden beams.

Reaching into his coat pocket Dennis extracted his lighter and flicked it on. The flame was slight but provided enough light for Dennis to navigate his way down the groaning wooden stairs, which bowed perilously under the soles of his work boots.

"Beth?"

Whatever had been burrowing into Branch's dirt floor must've been labouring for months. A throat-like tunnel yawned open just a few feet from where Dennis stood. Surrounding this opening was a puddle of something that shimmered when Dennis passed his Zippo over it. The fluid looked too thick to be water. It glistened like the slime left behind by a slug or a snail.

A whimper leaked out of the pit. Dennis' heart flung itself into the back of his throat. He stepped off the final stair and crouched by the opening. To Dennis' eye it looked as though something had actually dug its way *into* the house rather than escaping out of it.

The slowly shrinking flame wasn't enough to pierce the darkness of the pit. Something in the hole rustled and Dennis impulsively scurried back.

His palm sank into the cold sludge on the floor. The puddle was thick, lumpy, odourless. The Zippo had landed on the ground but its flame continued to burn.

Dennis snatched it up, hissing when the fire singed his fingertips. He was about to rise when he caught a reflection of himself within the rancid pool. At first Dennis was unsure as to what it was about the reflected image that paralyzed him with fear. Glinting stars popped and wobbled within the strange jelly. Dennis leaned in and squinted in deep concentration, trying to give form and identity to what he imagined he saw skulking in the slime.

Visions suddenly erupted in Dennis' mind. The dank walls of the cellar were usurped by vast landscapes of deserts with coarse black sands. Fledgling mountains fumed in the distance, jutting up like misshapen teeth against the hellfire glow of a bloody sky.

Weird flora lilted in the hot winds that now pushed Dennis across the sprawling terrain. He felt weightless, unbound. Faster and faster he glided over the Mesozoic plain, over howling behemoths and bubbling tar pits, past caves whose walls were adorned with strange alphabets scratched on with flint rock or smeared with the blood of the hunt.

He came upon a dim valley. Creatures that were no longer reptiles yet not quite avian fluttered their leathery wings and screeched from their perches. Below Dennis spotted several creatures fleeing, squawking and grunting. A tribe, he thought. Early men. Proto-humans. Their shaggy limbs pushing them up the crumbling wall of volcanic ash and out of this cauldron of shadows. One of the figures, a straggler, failed to scrabble up the crumbling incline. His slid hopelessly back down. Shrill, scratchy screams of terror tore loose from the thing's wide throat. His jaundiced eyes were wide with terror.

Then Dennis saw them. They came spilling out from the mouths of obscured caverns. Dwarvish things, black and hunched and hissing. There were five shapes that Dennis could see. More of them were surely lurking in the darkness, watching. Some of the creatures' bodies were covered in coarse greenish fur, others had scaly black hides. They were winged, they were barb-tailed. They were part-serpent, part-baboon. They were grey-eyed and fanged.

And they were speaking to each other.

Dennis did not hear their voices so much as he *felt* them. Their hissed, barbarous words shot through his body like surges of electricity.

The cabal swarmed around the fallen proto-human. Dennis wondered why the poor thing didn't fight. Surely his instinct to survive must've been great to last in such an era. But dread seemed to have paralyzed the straggler, for he now could not even grunt. His broad mouth hung slack as the chattering things slithered around him, forming a widdershins circle; a circle that began to open. A great pit, like a throat in the earth, stretched open, swallowing the man. It was into this pit that Dennis watched the dark things escape into.

And then he himself felt the ground disappearing all around him. Dennis was falling, changing, becoming ...

*   *   *

After refolding the envelope and sealing it with fresh tape, Beth hid the letter amongst her crosswords and volumes of trivia. She suddenly felt a sharp, acute stab of loneliness. Her chest felt cold and hollow; no doubt a side-effect of her own guilty conscience.

She was relieved when she spotted Dennis making his way up the front lawn. He was hunched low to the ground and trotting backwards, probably to shield himself from the harsh wind. Two hot Monte Cristo coffees seemed to be in order.

Beth pushed herself back from her desk.

There came a frantic scratching at the back door. It startled Beth. She called out her husband's name and a tear streamed down her right cheek.

A heartbeat later the house's threshold was breached.

Our dream was as firmly rooted in *Walden* as it was in Poe and Lovecraft. True, the grim fabulists, the macabre word-sorcerers, continually doused our mind-fires with fresh fuel, but it was Thoreau's memoir of escape and independence that truly lent form to our ambitions. The Gothic fed our dream, but it took a naturalist to provide us with a plan.

The initial idea had been Tanith's. Of course my wife had not been born with the name Tanith, any more than I was christened Thorn upon emerging from the womb, but we took these names (along with the surname Nightshade) to strengthen our vision and to better define who ... or rather *what* ... we were. These were our true names but they were ones that we kept secret from the world.

For months Tanith had been having a recurring dream involving a secluded house in the woods. It was as if her unconscious was guiding her on a room-by-room survey of her future. She began to keep a dream journal (a thick diary with a Moroccan goat leather cover) on our bedside table. I quickly grew accustomed to the whisper-hiss sound of her pen feverishly recording some new detail about our dream-house in the dead of night.

We talked endlessly about the house. We envisioned nights where the two of us would lock ourselves away behind black, foreboding doors. Tanith would do nothing but paint or compose elegiac music on a harpsichord, while I would add stanzas to my Great Poem, the one that was destined to stand alongside Dante's and Milton's as a timeless ode to darkness. We would wander the edge of a mist-padded tarn, or set offerings of tiny cakes and polished trinkets upon the large stone altar we'd erect to honour the night goddess. Our séance room would be open nightly to our select circle of friends. Every All Hallows Eve we would host an outdoor masquerade.

These were the aspirations that sustained us as we eked-out dreary routines of punch clocks, bills, and lunch meetings with clients. Our lives were ones of quiet desperation.

Beltane eve was the night we finally pledged an Oath that we would give our visions flesh.

It would take time, we knew. A great deal of time. And money. Oh so much money. Tanith and I listed the required sacrifices, weighed them, and ultimately accepted them.

For many years I continued to don the suit-and-tie uniform, and she the mask of the tough-as-nails business woman. We each toiled in shimmering high-rise office towers (the Ninth Circle of the post-modern age). We carried cell phones, worked ludicrous hours; all the while squirreling-away every penny we could spare. Tanith worked her fiscal magic, teaching me how to scrape-by on just a few dollars a day and yet never appear to be wanting.

A two-room apartment was our home through all those years. We lived on instant noodles, white bread, and tea. But our savings grew. And after an eternity, we were nearly free.

The hunt for our ideal property began.

We found a sympathetic real estate agent through Tanith's work. It took her well over a year, but in the end she found the nearest thing the material world had to my love's and my fantasy.

It was a farmhouse whose design was a chimerical blend of American Gothic and English Tudor. The property was an hour's drive from the city. It sat at the end of a muddy lane, guarded by rowan trees and cedars.

Tanith and I knew that taking on such a rustic property would require learning and labour. We would have to decipher the workings of a well and cistern, and get used to walking several kilometres into town anytime we needed provisions that were beyond the meagre harvest we would grow ourselves.

But our land was framed by an ancient stone wall, and there were towering oaks, a small marsh where toads and lightning bugs made their home. The house itself had some wrought-iron fixtures, a root cellar, and spire-capped cupolas on the roof. The real estate agent even mentioned that there were local rumours of a ghost that lurked the crumbling barn at the edge of our yard. We were home.

*   *   *

Following the purchase of the property, Tanith's and my life was sucked into a whirl of contractors and backbreaking repairs. We lugged countless cartons, sold-off almost all of our possessions, and learned how to till the soil.

In the end we had, at long last, withdrawn wholly from the modern age.

Summer scorched us, and autumn was an exhausting season of reaping the vegetables that we were forced to live on through the mercilessly cold winter. But we also wrote. And painted. We built redbrick altars in our yard and lived nocturnally during the off-seasons. Tanith lived up to her divine namesake by learning all manner of charm-crafting and incantations. We came to know the ghost in our barn rather well (an old farmhand who in life had been known as Gideon Walker).

Every two weeks or so we would walk into town to purchase essentials. At first we relished the glares and gasps that the appearance of black-clad bush-folk whose spindly bodies dangled with crude stone amulets and animal bones would conjure from the locals. But in time our life (for Tanith and I were now wed wholly into *one* life) became so insular and focused that my bride and I became the only people on Earth. I say we were the only *people*, but Tanith and I were certainly not alone. Our house was frequented by wraiths and neglected gods—the advantage of keeping our door (physical and otherwise) forever open.

Doubtless we were mad; deliriously, intoxicatingly insane.

*   *   *

It was November. A day of gravel-grey clouds, drizzle, gloom. Tanith had set out into the trees, armed with sheets of onion paper and a chunk of coal. Deep in the woods sat the ruins of a cemetery. Tanith went there often to meditate, to commune with the long-dead settlers of this land, or to preserve the wind-smoothed designs of their crumbling headstones with coal rubbings. I was occupied chopping wood for our winter stockpile that day. I didn't say goodbye.

Nightfall did not hold its usual allure for me; instead it found me standing on the porch, gazing into the darkness. An icy pressure swelled in the pit of my stomach. The lantern glowing at my side did nothing to ease the dampness or pierce the shadows. Periodically I would shatter the weighty silence by shouting Tanith's name. I must have sounded like a madman, especially when I began to stagger through the pitch-night.

The mud tried to hold me in place and the tree branches (which, stripped of their foliage, appeared petrified and menacing) sliced at the flesh of my face and groping hands.

My lantern burned dry, but my resolve was too strong. I felt my way through the lightless brush, stumbling deeper into the wild. I called Tanith's name until my shredded throat forbade it.

Dawn was leaking into the sky by the time I ventured back home. After staggering over what seemed to be an endless terrain, the edge of my property came into view.

I had hoped that my eyes would be met with some sign that my love had returned and was now keeping watch for me. But even from a distance I could see that our house was empty and dim.

A sense of helplessness mingled with raw panic. I felt hollowed-out. Forcing my legs to carry me back to the house was an almost impossible chore.

Staggering into the living room, I lit a fire in the hearth, sat on the floor, and sobbed. I'm not sure how long I rocked back and forth before the crackling flames, arms wrapped around bent knees in a feeble gesture of self-consolation.

I began to drift. My mind and body conspired to pull me, unwillingly, toward sleep.

I decided that I would rest, but only briefly. Then I would gather some supplies and begin searching for Tanith. I would not stop until I found her. If there was still no sign of her by midday I would seek help from the town.

She *would* come back to me. I was certain of it. I somehow managed to trick myself into a semi-relaxed state.

*   *   *

The sound of footsteps outside the house roused me. I could not have been asleep for long, for the sun was still rising above the trees in the east.

I sprung to my feet. The fire in the hearth had been reduced to a pile of steaming ash. Through the arched windows I saw strange splatters of light; ice-blue and panic-red, which lent my living room an otherworldly illumination. The knocker on the front door clunked, but I refused to answer it at first. I just stood shaking my head, like a child who shuts his eyes in order to make himself feel invisible, invincible.

I accidentally kicked a fallen book on my hesitant walk toward the entrance. A Bosch devil giggled at me from the opened volume as I opened the door.

Two uniformed police officers glared at me, accusingly it seemed at first, from my front porch. The sleek cruiser that was parked at the head of the lane looked positively incongruous on our antiquated property.

Almost unwittingly, I stepped outside to join the officers on my porch and was then piled into the back of their cruiser.

A few of the men and women in the sheriff's office insulted me about my appearance, my stench, my choice of lifestyle. Some were utterly unsympathetic, even after I gave a positive identification to the pale and broken cadaver they had lying on the slab.

In time I was given the details:

The groundskeeper of the old cemetery had found Tanith at dawn. Her body had been tossed into the ravine near the cemetery gates and had been hastily camouflaged with tree bark and leaves. She'd been raped by at least three different men. They'd broken her jaw, slashed her over forty times with what they suspect was a buck knife, before finally strangling her with the black velvet dress they'd stripped from her body.

The authorities suspected that a group of out-of-town campers (they assured me that this could not have been perpetrated by any of the locals) had done the deed and then disappeared into the night.

The subsequent investigation was fruitless. The sheriff suggested after some time had passed that I move on with my life, perhaps even leave town.

I was lost. I remember almost nothing of the weeks after I spread Tanith's cremated remains around our water well. I sold the property and eventually returned to the city.

131

*   *   *

I'm currently working as a dishwasher in a restaurant in order to pay my rent on a one-bedroom apartment here in the city. Though I'm qualified for a far more challenging and lucrative vocation, I cannot bring myself to do it. All my aspirations were left slashed and mutilated in the night woods.

I've discovered little ways to fill my spare time. I take long walks, do jigsaw puzzles. On Sunday mornings I will often go to church. I find the sermons punitive, and that's good.

Worse than the pain and loss is the bitter irony of our fate. It chokes me every time I think of it.

The irony is that Tanith and I had spent our lives evoking the horrors … and in the end the horrors heeded.

THE TALES OF INSPECTOR LEGRASSE

H. P. LOVECRAFT & C. J. HENDERSON

AVAILABLE TO ORDER
www.mythosbooks.com

UNHOLY DIMENSIONS

JEFFREY THOMAS

AVAILABLE TO ORDER
www.mythosbooks.com

THE LOVECRAFT CHRONICLES

PETER CANNON

AVAILABLE TO ORDER
www.mythosbooks.com

AVAILABLE TO ORDER
www.mythosbooks.com

Printed in the United States
96162LV00001B/4/A

9 780978 991128